Douglas Adams created all the various and contradictory manifestations of *The Hitchhiker's Guide to the Galaxy*: radio, novels, TV, computer game, stage adaptations, comic book and bath towel. A major movie is currently in development hell and will almost certainly be released any decade now. He lectured and broadcast around the world and was a patron of the Dian Fossey Gorilla Fund and Save the Rhino International.

He was born in Cambridge, UK and lived with his wife and daughter in Santa Barbara, California, where he died suddenly on 11 May 2001.

For more information, visit *www.douglasadams.com*

If you are interested in the works of Douglas Adams, you may like to join ZZ9 Plural Z Alpha, the official Hitchhiker's Guide to the Galaxy Appreciation Society, founded in 1980. For details of this fan-run club visit www.zz9.org or send a SAE/IRC to:

ZZ9 Plural Z Alpha
4 The Sycamores, Hadfield
Derbyshire, SK13 2BS, UK

by the same author

The Hitchhiker series:

The Hitchhiker's Guide to the Galaxy
The Restaurant at the End of the Universe
Life, the Universe and Everything
So Long, and Thanks for all the Fish
Mostly Harmless

The Dirk Gently series:

Dirk Gently's Holistic Detective Agency
The Long Dark Tea-time of the Soul

With John Lloyd:

The Meaning of Liff
The Deeper Meaning of Liff

With Mark Carwardine:

Last Chance to See . . .

By Terry Jones, based on a story/
computer game by Douglas Adams:

Starship Titanic

DOUGLAS ADAMS

Life, the Universe and Everything

Pan Books

First published 1982 by Pan Books
an imprint of Pan Macmillan Ltd
Pan Macmillan, 20 New Wharf Road, London N1 9RR
Basingstoke and Oxford
Associated companies throughout the world
www.panmacmillan.com

ISBN-13: 978-0-330-26738-0
ISBN-10: 0-330-26738-8

62

A CIP catalogue record for this book is available from the British Library.

Typeset by SetSystems Ltd, Saffron Walden, Essex
Printed and bound in Great Britain by
Mackays of Chatham plc, Chatham, Kent

for Sally

1

The regular early morning yell of horror was the sound of Arthur Dent waking up and suddenly remembering where he was.

It wasn't just that the cave was cold, it wasn't just that it was damp and smelly. It was the fact that the cave was in the middle of Islington and there wasn't a bus due for two million years.

Time is the worst place, so to speak, to get lost in, as Arthur Dent could testify, having been lost in both time and space a good deal. At least being lost in space kept you busy.

He was stranded in prehistoric Earth as the result of a complex sequence of events which had involved him being alternately blown up and insulted in more bizarre regions of the Galaxy than he had ever dreamt existed, and though life had now turned very, very, very quiet, he was still feeling jumpy.

He hadn't been blown up now for five years.

Since he had hardly seen anyone since he and Ford Prefect had parted company four years previously, he hadn't been insulted in all that time either.

Except just once.

It had happened on a spring evening about two years previously.

He was returning to his cave just a little after dusk when he became aware of lights flashing eerily through the clouds. He turned and stared, with hope suddenly clambering through his heart. Rescue. Escape. The castaway's impossible dream – a ship.

And as he watched, as he stared in wonder and excitement, a long silver ship descended through the warm evening air, quietly, without fuss, its long legs unlocking in a smooth ballet of technology.

It alighted gently on the ground, and what little hum it had generated died away, as if lulled by the evening calm.

A ramp extended itself.

Light streamed out.

A tall figure appeared silhouetted in the hatchway. It walked down the ramp and stood in front of Arthur.

'You're a jerk, Dent,' it said simply.

It was alien, very alien. It had a peculiar alien tallness, a peculiar alien flattened head, peculiar slitty little alien eyes, extravagantly draped golden robes with a peculiarly alien collar design, and pale grey-green alien skin which had about it that lustrous sheen which most grey-green faces can only acquire with plenty of exercise and very expensive soap.

Arthur boggled at it.

It gazed levelly at him.

Arthur's first sensations of hope and trepidation had instantly been overwhelmed by astonishment, and all sorts of thoughts were battling for the use of his vocal cords at this moment.

'Whh . . . ?' he said.

'Bu . . . hu . . . uh . . .' he added.

'Ru . . . ra . . . wah . . . who?' he managed finally to say and lapsed into a frantic kind of silence. He was feeling the effects of having not said anything to anybody for as long as he could remember.

The alien creature frowned briefly and consulted what appeared to be some species of clipboard which he was holding in his thin and spindly alien hand.

'Arthur Dent?' it said.

Arthur nodded helplessly.

'Arthur *Philip* Dent?' pursued the alien in a kind of efficient yap.

'Er . . . er . . . yes . . . er . . . er,' confirmed Arthur.

'You're a jerk,' repeated the alien, 'a complete asshole.'

'Er . . .'

The creature nodded to itself, made a peculiar alien tick on its clipboard and turned briskly back towards its ship.

'Er . . .' said Arthur desperately, 'er . . .'

'Don't give me that,' snapped the alien. It marched up the ramp, through the hatchway and disappeared into its ship. The ship sealed itself. It started to make a low throbbing hum.

'Er, hey!' shouted Arthur, and started to run helplessly towards it.

'Wait a minute!' he called. 'What is this? What? Wait a minute!'

The ship rose, as if shedding its weight like a cloak to the ground, and hovered briefly. It swept strangely up into the evening sky. It passed up through the clouds, illuminating them briefly, and then was gone, leaving Arthur alone in an immensity of land dancing a helplessly tiny little dance.

'What?' he screamed. 'What? What? Hey, what? Come back here and say that!'

He jumped and danced until his legs trembled, and shouted till his lungs rasped. There was no answer from anyone. There was no one to hear him or speak to him.

The alien ship was already thundering towards the upper reaches of the atmosphere, on its way out into the appalling void which separates the very few things there are in the Universe from each other.

Its occupant, the alien with the expensive complexion,

leaned back in its single seat. His name was Wowbagger the Infinitely Prolonged. He was a man with a purpose. Not a very good purpose, as he would have been the first to admit, but it was at least a purpose and it did at least keep him on the move.

Wowbagger the Infinitely Prolonged was – indeed, is – one of the Universe's very small number of immortal beings.

Those who are born immortal instinctively know how to cope with it, but Wowbagger was not one of them. Indeed he had come to hate them, the load of serene bastards. He had had his immortality inadvertently thrust upon him by an unfortunate accident with an irrational particle accelerator, a liquid lunch and a pair of rubber bands. The precise details of the accident are not important because no one has ever managed to duplicate the exact circumstances under which it happened, and many people have ended up looking very silly, or dead, or both, trying.

Wowbagger closed his eyes in a grim and weary expression, put some light jazz on the ship's stereo, and reflected that he could have made it if it hadn't been for Sunday afternoons, he really could have done.

To begin with it was fun, he had a ball, living dangerously, taking risks, cleaning up on high-yield long-term investments, and just generally outliving the hell out of everybody.

In the end, it was the Sunday afternoons he couldn't cope with, and that terrible listlessness which starts to set in at about 2.55, when you know that you've had all the baths you can usefully have that day, that however hard you stare at any given paragraph in the papers you will never actually read it, or use the revolutionary new pruning technique it describes, and that as you stare at the clock the hands will move relentlessly on to four o'clock, and you will enter the long dark teatime of the soul.

So things began to pall for him. The merry smiles he used to wear at other people's funerals began to fade. He began to despise the Universe in general and everybody in it in particular.

This was the point at which he conceived his purpose, the thing which would drive him on, and which, as far as he could see, would drive him on for ever. It was this.

He would insult the Universe.

That is, he would insult everybody in it. Individually, personally, one by one, and (this was the thing he really decided to grit his teeth over) in alphabetical order.

When people protested to him, as they sometimes had done, that the plan was not merely misguided but actually impossible because of the number of people being born and dying all the time, he would merely fix them with a steely look and say, 'A man can dream, can't he?'

And so he had started out. He equipped a spaceship that was built to last with a computer capable of handling all the data processing involved in keeping track of the entire population of the known Universe and working out the horrifically complicated routes involved.

His ship fled through the inner orbits of the Sol star system, preparing to slingshot round the sun and fling itself out into interstellar space.

'Computer,' he said.

'Here,' yipped the computer.

'Where next?'

'Computing that.'

Wowbagger gazed for a moment at the fantastic jewellery of the night, the billions of tiny diamond worlds that dusted the infinite darkness with light. Every one, every single one, was on his itinerary. Most of them he would be going to millions of times over.

He imagined for a moment his itinerary connecting up all the dots in the sky like a child's numbered dots puzzle. He hoped that from some vantage point in the Universe it might be seen to spell a very very rude word.

The computer beeped tunelessly to indicate that it had finished its calculations.

'Folfanga,' it said. It beeped.

'Fourth world of the Folfanga system,' it continued. It beeped again.

'Estimated journey time, three weeks,' it continued further. It beeped again.

'There to meet with a small slug,' it beeped, 'of the genus A-Rth-Urp-Hil-Ipdenu.'

'I believe,' it added, after a slight pause during which it beeped, 'that you had decided to call it a brainless prat.'

Wowbagger grunted. He watched the majesty of creation outside his window for a moment or two.

'I think I'll take a nap,' he said, and then added, 'what network areas are we going to be passing through in the next few hours?'

The computer beeped.

'Cosmovid, Thinkpix and Home Brain Box,' it said, and beeped.

'Any movies I haven't seen thirty thousand times already?'

'No.'

'Uh.'

'There's *Angst in Space*. You've only seen that thirty-three thousand five hundred and seventeen times.'

'Wake me for the second reel.'

The computor beeped.

'Sleep well,' it said.

The ship fled on through the night.

Meanwhile, on Earth, it began to pour with rain and Arthur Dent sat in his cave and had one of the most truly rotten evenings of his entire life, thinking of things he could have said to the alien and swatting flies, who also had a rotten evening.

The next day he made himself a pouch out of rabbit skin because he thought it would be useful to keep things in.

2

This morning, two years later than that, was sweet and fragrant as he emerged from the cave he called home until he could think of a better name for it or find a better cave.

Though his throat was sore again from his early morning yell of horror, he was suddenly in a terrifically good mood. He wrapped his dilapidated dressing gown tightly around him and beamed at the bright morning.

The air was clear and scented, the breeze flitted lightly through the tall grass around his cave, the birds were chirruping at each other, the butterflies were flitting about prettily, and the whole of nature seemed to be conspiring to be as pleasant as it possibly could.

It wasn't all the pastoral delights that were making Arthur feel so cheery, though. He had just had a wonderful idea about how to cope with the terrible lonely isolation, the nightmares, the failure of all his attempts at horticulture, and the sheer futurelessness and futility of his life here on prehistoric Earth, which was that he would go mad.

He beamed again and took a bite out of a rabbit leg left over from his supper. He chewed happily for a few moments and then decided formally to announce his decision.

He stood up straight and looked the world squarely in the fields and hills. To add weight to his words he stuck the rabbit bone in his hair. He spread his arms out wide.

'I will go mad!' he announced.

'Good idea,' said Ford Prefect, clambering down from the rock on which he had been sitting.

Arthur's brain somersaulted. His jaw did press-ups.

'I went mad for a while,' said Ford, 'did me no end of good.'

Arthur's eyes did cartwheels.

'You see,' said Ford, '– . . .'

'Where have you been?' interrupted Arthur, now that his head had finished working out.

'Around,' said Ford, 'around and about.' He grinned in what he accurately judged to be an infuriating manner. 'I just took my mind off the hook for a bit. I reckoned that if the world wanted me badly enough it would call back. It did.'

He took out of his now terribly battered and dilapidated satchel his Sub-Etha Sens-O-Matic.

'At least,' he said, 'I think it did. This has been playing up a bit.' He shook it. 'If it was a false alarm I shall go mad,' he said, 'again.'

Arthur shook his head and sat down. He looked up.

'I thought you must be dead . . .' he said simply.

'So did I for a while,' said Ford, 'and then I decided I was a lemon for a couple of weeks. I kept myself amused all that time jumping in and out of a gin and tonic.'

Arthur cleared his throat, and then did it again.

'Where,' he said, 'did you . . . ?'

'Find a gin and tonic?' said Ford brightly. 'I found a small lake that thought it was a gin and tonic, and jumped in and out of that. At least, I think it thought it was a gin and tonic.

'I may,' he added with a grin which would have sent sane men scampering into trees, 'have been imagining it.'

He waited for a reaction from Arthur, but Arthur knew better than that.

'Carry on,' he said evenly.

'The point is, you see,' said Ford, 'that there is no point in driving yourself mad trying to stop yourself going mad. You might just as well give in and save your sanity for later.'

'And this is you sane again, is it?' said Arthur. 'I ask merely for information.'

'I went to Africa,' said Ford.

'Yes?'

'Yes.'

'What was that like?'

'And this is your cave, is it?' said Ford.

'Er, yes,' said Arthur. He felt very strange. After nearly four years of total isolation he was so pleased and relieved to see Ford that he could almost cry. Ford was, on the other hand, an almost immediatetly annoying person.

'Very nice,' said Ford, in reference to Arthur's cave. 'You must hate it.'

Arthur didn't bother to reply.

'Africa was very interesting,' said Ford, 'I behaved very oddly there.'

He gazed thoughtfully into the distance.

'I took up being cruel to animals,' he said airily. 'But only,' he added, 'as a hobby.'

'Oh yes,' said Arthur, warily.

'Yes,' Ford assured him. 'I won't disturb you with the details because they would—'

'What?'

'Disturb you. But you may be interested to know that I am singlehandedly responsible for the evolved shape of the animal you came to know in later centuries as a giraffe. And I tried to learn to fly. Do you believe me?'

'Tell me,' said Arthur.

'I'll tell you later. I'll just mention that the *Guide* says . . .'

'The . . .?'

'*Guide. The Hitchhiker's Guide to the Galaxy.* You remember?'

'Yes. I remember throwing it in the river.'

'Yes,' said Ford, 'but I fished it out.'

'You didn't tell me.'

'I didn't want you to throw it in again.'

'Fair enough,' admitted Arthur. 'It says?'

'What?'

'The *Guide* says?'

'The *Guide* says that there is an art to flying,' said Ford, 'or rather a knack. The knack lies in learning how to throw yourself at the ground and miss.' He smiled weakly. He pointed at the knees of his trousers and held his arms up to show the elbows. They were all torn and worn through.

'I haven't done very well so far,' he said. He stuck out his hand. 'I'm very glad to see you again, Arthur,' he added.

Arthur shook his head in a sudden access of emotion and bewilderment.

'I haven't seen anyone for years,' he said, 'not anyone. I can hardly even remember how to speak. I keep forgetting words. I practise, you see. I practise by talking to . . . talking to . . . what are those things people think you're mad if you talk to? Like George the Third.'

'Kings?' suggested Ford.

'No, no,' said Arthur. 'The things he used to talk to. We're surrounded by them, for Heaven's sake. I've planted hundreds myself. They all died. Trees! I practise by talking to trees. What's that for?'

Ford still had his hand stuck out. Arthur looked at it with incomprehension.

'Shake,' prompted Ford.

Arthur did, nervously at first, as if it might turn out to be a fish. Then he grasped it vigorously with both hands in an overwhelming flood of relief. He shook it and shook it.

After a while Ford found it necessary to disengage. They climbed to the top of a nearby outcrop of rock and surveyed the scene around them.

'What happened to the Golgafrinchans?' asked Ford.

Arthur shrugged.

'A lot of them didn't make it through the winter three years ago,' he said, 'and the few who remained in the spring said they needed a holiday and set off on a raft. History says that they must have survived . . .'

'Huh,' said Ford, 'well well.' He stuck his hands on his hips and looked round again at the empty world. Suddenly, there was about Ford a sense of energy and purpose.

'We're going,' he said excitedly, and shivered with energy.

'Where? How?' said Arthur.

'I don't know,' said Ford, 'but I just feel that the time is right. Things are going to happen. We're on our way.'

He lowered his voice to a whisper.

'I have detected,' he said, 'disturbances in the wash.'

He gazed keenly into the distance and looked as if he would quite like the wind to blow his hair back dramatically at that point, but the wind was busy fooling around with some leaves a little way off.

Arthur asked him to repeat what he had just said because he hadn't quite taken his meaning. Ford repeated it.

'The wash?' said Arthur.

'The space–time wash,' said Ford, and as the wind blew briefly past at that moment, he bared his teeth into it.

Arthur nodded, and then cleared his throat.

'Are we talking about,' he asked cautiously, 'some sort of Vogon laundromat, or what are we talking about?'

'Eddies,' said Ford, 'in the space–time continuum.'

'Ah, nodded Arthur, 'is he? Is he?' He pushed his hands into the pocket of his dressing gown and looked knowledgeably into the distance.

'What?' said Ford.

'Er, who,' said Arthur, 'is Eddy, then, exactly, then?'

Ford looked angrily at him.

'Will you listen?' he snapped.

'I have been listening,' said Arthur, 'but I'm not sure it's helped.'

Ford grasped him by the lapels of his dressing gown and spoke to him as slowly and distinctly and patiently as if he were somebody from a telephone company accounts department.

'There seem . . .' he said, 'to be some pools . . .' he said, 'of instability . . .' he said, 'in the fabric . . .' he said . . .

Arthur looked foolishly at the cloth of his dressing

gown where Ford was holding it. Ford swept on before Arthur could turn the foolish look into a foolish remark.

'. . . in the fabric of space–time,' he said.

'Ah, that,' said Arthur.

'Yes, that,' confirmed Ford.

They stood there alone on a hill on prehistoric Earth and stared each other resolutely in the face.

'And it's done what?' said Arthur.

'It,' said Ford, 'has developed pools of instability.'

'Has it?' said Arthur, his eyes not wavering for a moment.

'It has,' said Ford with a similar degree of occular immobility.

'Good,' said Arthur.

'See?' said Ford.

'No,' said Arthur.

There was a quiet pause.

'The difficulty with this conversation,' said Arthur after a sort of pondering look had crawled slowly across his face like a mountaineer negotiating a tricky outcrop, 'is that it's very different from most of the ones I've had of late. Which, as I explained, have mostly been with trees. They weren't like this. Except perhaps some of the ones I've had with elms which sometimes get a bit bogged down.'

'Arthur,' said Ford.

'Hello? Yes?' said Arthur.

'Just believe everything I tell you, and it will all be very very simple.'

'Ah, well I'm not sure I believe that.'

They sat down and composed their thoughts.

Ford got out his Sub-Etha Sens-O-Matic. It was making vague humming noises and a tiny light on it was flickering faintly.

'Flat battery?' said Arthur.

'No,' said Ford, 'there is a moving disturbance in the fabric of space–time, an eddy, a pool of instability, and it's somewhere in our vicinity.'

'Where?'

Ford moved the device in a slow, lightly bobbing semi-circle. Suddenly the light flashed.

'There!' said Ford, shooting out his arm. 'There, behind that sofa!'

Arthur looked. Much to his surprise, there was a velvet-paisley-covered Chesterfield sofa in the field in front of them. He boggled intelligently at it. Shrewd questions sprang into his mind.

'Why,' he said, 'is there a sofa in that field?'

'I told you!' shouted Ford, leaping to his feet. 'Eddies in the space–time continuum!'

'And this is his sofa, is it?' asked Arthur, struggling to his feet and, he hoped, though not very optimistically, to his senses.

'Arthur!' shouted Ford at him. 'That sofa is there because of the space–time instability I've been trying to get your terminally softened brain to get to grips with. It's been washed up out of the continuum, it's space–time jetsam, it doesn't matter what it is, we've got to catch it, it's our only way out of here!'

He scrambled rapidly down the rocky outcrop and made off across the field.

'Catch it?' muttered Arthur, then frowned in bemusement as he saw that the Chesterfield was lazily bobbing and wafting away across the grass.

With a whoop of utterly unexpected delight he leapt down the rock and plunged off in hectic pursuit of Ford Prefect and the irrational piece of furniture.

They careered wildly through the grass, leaping, laughing, shouting instructions to each other to head the thing off this way or that way. The sun shone dreamily on the swaying grass, tiny field animals scattered crazily in their wake.

Arthur felt happy. He was terribly pleased that the day was for once working out so much according to plan. Only twenty minutes ago he had decided he would go mad, and now here he was already chasing a sofa across the fields of prehistoric Earth.

The sofa bobbed this way and that and seemed simultaneously to be as solid as the trees as it drifted past some of them and hazy as a billowing dream as it floated like a ghost through others.

Ford and Arthur pounded chaotically after it, but it dodged and weaved as if following its own complex mathematical topography, which it was. Still they pursued, still it danced and span, and suddenly turned and dipped as if crossing the lip of a catastrophe graph, and they were practically on top of it. With a heave and a shout they kept on it, the sun winked out, they fell through a sickening nothingness, and emerged unexpectedly in the middle of the pitch at Lord's Cricket Ground, St John's Wood, London, towards the end of the last Test Match of the Australian Series in the year 198—, with England needing only twenty-eight runs to win.

3

Important facts from Galactic history, number one:
(Reproduced from the *Siderial Daily Mentioner's Book of Popular Galactic History*.)

The night sky over the planet Krikkit is the least interesting sight in the entire Universe.

4

It was a charming and delightful day at Lord's as Ford and Arthur tumbled haphazardly out of a space–time anomaly and hit the immaculate turf rather hard.

The applause of the crowd was tremendous. It wasn't for them, but instinctively they bowed anyway, which was fortunate because the small red heavy ball which the crowd actually had been applauding whistled mere millimetres over Arthur's head. In the crowd a man collapsed.

They threw themselves back to the ground which seemed to spin hideously around them.

'What was that?' hissed Arthur.

'Something red,' hissed Ford back at him.

'Where are we?'

'Er, somewhere green.'

'Shapes,' muttered Arthur. 'I need shapes.'

The applause of the crowd had been rapidly succeeded by gasps of astonishment, and the awkward titters of hundreds of people who could not yet make up their minds about whether to believe what they had just seen or not.

'This your sofa?' said a voice.

'What was that?' whispered Ford.

Arthur looked up.

'Something blue,' he said.

'Shape?' said Ford.

Arthur looked again.

'It is shaped,' he hissed at Ford, with his brow savagely furrowed, 'like a policeman.'

They remained crouched there for a few moments, frowning deeply. The blue thing shaped like a policeman tapped them both on the shoulders.

'Come on, you two,' the shape said, 'let's be having you.'

These words had an electrifying effect on Arthur. He leapt to his feet like an author hearing the phone ring and shot a series of startled glances at the panorama around him which had suddenly settled down into something of quite terrifying ordinariness.

'Where did you get this from?' he yelled at the policeman shape.

'What did you say?' said the startled shape.

'This is Lord's Cricket Ground, isn't it?' snapped Arthur. 'Where did you find it, how did you get it here? I think,' he added, clasping his hand to his brow, 'that I had better calm down.' He squatted down abruptly in front of Ford.

'It is a policeman,' he said. 'What do we do?'

Ford shrugged.

'What do you want to do?' he said.

'I want you,' said Arthur, 'to tell me that I have been dreaming for the last five years.'

Ford shrugged again, and obliged.

'You've been dreaming for the last five years,' he said.

Arthur got to his feet.

'It's all right officer,' he said. 'I've been dreaming for the last five years. Ask him,' he added, pointing at Ford, 'he was in it.'

Having said this, he sauntered off towards the edge of the pitch, brushing down his dressing gown. He then noticed his dressing gown and stopped. He stared at it. He flung himself at the policeman.

'So where did I get these clothes from?' he howled.

He collapsed and lay twitching on the grass.

Ford shook his head.

'He's had a bad two million years,' he said to the policeman, and together they heaved Arthur on to the sofa and carried him off the pitch and were only briefly hampered by the sudden disappearance of the sofa on the way.

Reactions to all this from the crowd were many and various. Most of them couldn't cope with watching it, and listened to it on the radio instead.

'Well, this is an interesting incident, Brian,' said one radio commentator to another. 'I don't think there have been any mysterious materializations on the pitch since, oh since, well I don't think there have been any – have there? – that I recall?'

'Edgbaston, 1932?'

'Ah, now what happened then . . .?'

'Well, Peter, I think it was Canter facing Willcox coming up to bowl from the pavilion end when a spectator suddenly ran straight across the pitch.'

There was a pause whilst the first commentator considered this.

'Ye . . . e . . . s . . .' he said, 'yes, there's nothing actually very mysterious about that, is there? He didn't actually materialize, did he? Just ran on.'

'No, that's true, but he did claim to have *seen* something materialize on the pitch.'

'Ah, did he?'

'Yes. An alligator, I think, of some description.'

'Ah. And had anyone else noticed it?'

'Apparently not. And no one was able to get a very detailed description from him, so only the most perfunctory search was made.'

'And what happened to the man?'

'Well, I think someone offered to take him off and give him some lunch but he explained that he'd already had a rather good one, so the matter was dropped and Warwickshire went on to win by three wickets.'

'So, not very like this current instance. For those of you who've just tuned in, you may be interested to know that, er . . . two men, two rather scruffily attired men, and indeed a sofa – a Chesterfield, I think?'

'Yes, a Chesterfield.'

'Have just materialized here in the middle of Lord's Cricket Ground. But I don't think they meant any harm, they've been very good-natured about it, and—'

'Sorry, can I interrupt you a moment, Peter, and say that the sofa has just vanished.'

'So it has. Well, that's one mystery less. Still, it's definitely one for the record books, I think, particularly occuring at this dramatic moment in play, England now needing only twenty-four runs to win the series. The men are leaving the pitch in the company of a police officer, and I think everyone's settling down now and play is about to resume.'

'Now, sir,' said the policeman after they had made a passage through the curious crowd and laid Arthur's peacefully inert body on a blanket, 'perhaps you'd care to tell me who you are, where you come from, and what that little scene was all about?'

Ford looked at the ground for a moment as if steadying himself for something, then he straightened up and aimed a look at the policeman which hit him with the full force of every inch of the six light-years' distance between Earth and Ford's home near Betelgeuse.

'All right,' said Ford, very quietly, 'I'll tell you.'

'Yes, well, that won't be necessary,' said the policeman hurriedly, 'just don't let whatever it was happen again.' The policeman turned around and wandered off in search of anyone who wasn't from Betelgeuse. Fortunately, the ground was full of them.

Arthur's consciousness approached his body as from a great distance, and reluctantly. It had had some bad times in there. Slowly, nervously, it entered and settled down in to its accustomed position.

Arthur sat up.

'Where am I?' he said.

'Lord's Cricket Ground,' said Ford.

'Fine,' said Arthur, and his consciousness stepped out again for a quick breather. His body flopped back on the grass.

Ten minutes later, hunched over a cup of tea in the refreshment tent, the colour started to come back to his haggard face.

'How're you feeling?' said Ford.

'I'm home,' said Arthur hoarsely. He closed his eyes and greedily inhaled the steam from his tea as if it was – well, as far as Arthur was concerned, as if it was tea, which it was.

'I'm home,' he repeated, 'home. It's England, it's today, the nightmare is over.' He opened his eyes again and smiled serenely. 'I'm where I belong,' he said in an emotional whisper.

'There are two things I feel I should tell you,' said Ford, tossing a copy of the *Guardian* over the table at him.

'I'm home,' said Arthur.

'Yes,' said Ford. 'One is,' he said pointing at the date at the top of the paper, 'that the Earth will be demolished in two days' time.'

'I'm home,' said Arthur. 'Tea,' he said, 'cricket,' he added with pleasure, 'mown grass, wooden benches, white linen jackets, beer cans . . .'

Slowly he began to focus on the newspaper. He cocked his head on one side with a slight frown.

'I've seen that one before,' he said. His eyes wandered slowly up to the date, which Ford was idly tapping at. His face froze for a second or two and then began to do that terribly slow crashing trick which Arctic ice-floes do so spectacularly in the spring.

'And the other thing,' said Ford, 'is that you appear to have a bone in your beard.' He tossed back his tea.

Outside the refreshment tent, the sun was shining on a happy crowd. It shone on white hats and red faces. It shone on ice lollies and melted them. It shone on the tears of small children whose ice lollies had just melted and fallen off the stick. It shone on the trees, it flashed off whirling cricket bats, it gleamed off the utterly extraordinary object which was parked behind the sight-screens and which nobody appeared to have noticed. It beamed on Ford and Arthur as they emerged blinking from the refreshment tent and surveyed the scene around them.

Arthur was shaking.

'Perhaps,' he said, 'I should . . .'

'No,' said Ford sharply.

'What?' said Arthur.

'Don't try and phone yourself up at home.'

'How did you know . . . ?'

Ford shrugged.

'But why not?' said Arthur.

'People who talk to themselves on the phone,' said Ford, 'never learn anything to their advantage.'

'But . . .'

'Look,' said Ford. He picked up an imaginary phone and dialled an imaginary dial.

'Hello?' he said into the imaginary mouthpiece. 'Is

that Arthur Dent? Ah, hello, yes. This is Arthur Dent speaking. Don't hang up.'

He looked at the imaginary phone in disappointment.

'He hung up,' he said, shrugged, and put the imaginary phone neatly back on its imaginary hook.

'This is not my first temporal anomaly,' he added.

A glummer look replaced the already glum look on Arthur Dent's face.

'So we're not home and dry,' he said.

'We could not even be said,' replied Ford, 'to be home and vigorously towelling ourselves off.'

The game continued. The bowler approached the wicket at a lope, a trot, and then a run. He suddenly exploded in a flurry of arms and legs, out of which flew a ball. The batsman swung and thwacked it behind him over the sight-screens. Ford's eyes followed the trajectory of the ball and jagged momentarily. He stiffened. He looked along the flight path of the ball again and his eyes twitched again.

'This isn't my towel,' said Arthur, who was rummaging in his rabbit-skin bag.

'Shhh,' said Ford. He screwed his eyes up in concentration.

'I had a Golgafrinchan jogging towel,' continued Arthur, 'it was blue with yellow stars on it. This isn't it.'

'Shhh,' said Ford again. He covered one eye and looked with the other.

'This one's pink,' said Arthur, 'it isn't yours, is it?'

'I would like you to shut up about your towel,' said Ford.

'It isn't my towel,' insisted Arthur, 'that is the point I am trying to . . .'

'And the time at which I would like you to shut up about it,' continued Ford in a low growl, 'is now.'

'All right,' said Arthur, starting to stuff it back into

the primitively stitched rabbit-skin bag. 'I realize that it is probably not important in the cosmic scale of things, it's just odd, that's all. A pink towel suddenly, instead of a blue one with yellow stars.'

Ford was beginning to behave rather strangely, or rather not actually beginning to behave strangely but beginning to behave in a way which was strangely different from the other strange ways in which he more regularly behaved. What he was doing was this. Regardless of the bemused stares it was provoking from his fellow members of the crowd gathered round the pitch, he was waving his hands in sharp movements across his face, ducking down behind some people, leaping up behind others, then standing still and blinking a lot. After a moment or two of this he started to stalk forward slowly and stealthily wearing a puzzled frown of concentration, like a leopard that is not sure whether it's just seen a half-empty tin of cat food half a mile away across a hot and dusty plain.

'This isn't my bag either,' said Arthur suddenly.

Ford's spell of concentration was broken. He turned angrily on Arthur.

'I wasn't talking about my towel,' said Arthur. 'We've established that that isn't mine. It's just that the bag into which I was putting the towel which is not mine is also not mine, though it is extraordinarily similar. Now personally I think that that is extremely odd, especially as the bag was one I made myself on prehistoric Earth. These are also not my stones,' he added, pulling a few flat grey stones out of the bag. 'I was making a collection of interesting stones and these are clearly very dull ones.'

A roar of excitement thrilled through the crowd and obliterated whatever it was that Ford said in reply to this piece of information. The cricket ball which had excited this reaction fell out of the sky and dropped neatly into Arthur's mysterious rabbit-skin bag.

'Now I would say that that was also a very curious event,' said Arthur, rapidly closing the bag and pretending to look for the ball on the ground.

'I don't think it's here,' he said to the small boys who immediately clustered round him to join in the search, 'it probably rolled off somewhere. Over there I expect.' He pointed vaguely in the direction in which he wished they would push off. One of the boys looked at him quizzically.

'You all right?' said the boy.

'No,' said Arthur.

'Then why you got a bone in your beard?' said the boy.

'I'm training it to like being wherever it's put.' Arthur prided himself on saying this. It was, he thought, exactly the sort of thing which would entertain and stimulate young minds.

'Oh,' said the small boy, putting his head on one side and thinking about it. 'What's your name?'

'Dent,' said Arthur, 'Arthur Dent.'

'You're a jerk, Dent,' said the boy, 'a complete asshole.' The boy looked past him at something else, to show that he wasn't in any particular hurry to run away, and then wandered off scratching his nose. Suddenly Arthur remembered that the Earth was going to be demolished again in two days' time, and just this once didn't feel too bad about it.

Play resumed with a new ball, the sun continued to shine and Ford continued to jump up and down shaking his head and blinking.

'Something's on your mind, isn't it?' said Arthur.

'I think,' said Ford in a tone of voice which Arthur by

now recognized as one which presaged utterly unintelligible, 'that there's an SEP over there.'

He pointed. Curiously enough, the direction he pointed in was not the one in which he was looking. Arthur looked in the one direction, which was towards the sight-screens, and in the other which was at the field of play. He nodded, he shrugged. He shrugged again.

'A what?' he said.

'An SEP.'

'An S . . . ?'

'. . . EP.'

'And what's that?'

'Somebody Else's Problem,' said Ford.

'Ah, good,' said Arthur and relaxed. He had no idea what all that was about, but at best it seemed to be over. It wasn't.

'Over there,' said Ford, again pointing at the sight-screens and looking at the pitch.

'Where?' said Arthur.

'There!' said Ford.

'I see,' said Arthur, who didn't.

'You do?' said Ford.

'What?' said Arthur.

'Can you see,' said Ford patiently, 'the SEP?'

'I thought you said that was someone else's problem.'

'That's right.'

Arthur nodded slowly, carefully and with an air of immense cupidity.

'And I want to know,' said Ford, 'if you can see it.'

'You do?'

'Yes.'

'What,' said Arthur, 'does it look like?'

'Well, how should I know, you fool?' shouted Ford. 'If you can see it, you tell me.'

Arthur experienced that dull throbbing sensation just behind the temples which was a hallmark of so many of his conversations with Ford. His brain lurked like a frightened puppy in its kennel. Ford took him by the arm.

'An SEP,' he said, 'is something that we can't see, or don't see, or our brain doesn't let us see, because we think that it's somebody else's problem. That's what SEP means. Somebody Else's Problem. The brain just edits it out, it's like a blind spot. If you look at it directly you won't see it unless you know precisely what it is. Your only hope is to catch it by surprise out of the corner of your eye.'

'Ah,' said Arthur, 'then that's why . . .'

'Yes,' said Ford, who knew what Arthur was going to say.

'. . . you've been jumping up and . . .'

'Yes.'

'. . . down, and blinking . . .'

'Yes.'

'. . . and . . .'

'I think you've got the message.'

'I can see it,' said Arthur, 'it's a spaceship.'

For a moment Arthur was stunned by the reaction this revelation provoked. A roar erupted from the crowd, and from every direction people were running, shouting, yelling, tumbling over each other in a tumult of confusion. He stumbled back in astonishment and glanced fearfully around. Then he glanced around again in even greater astonishment.

'Exciting, isn't it?' said an apparition. The apparition wobbled in front of Arthur's eyes, though the truth of the matter is probably that Arthur's eyes were wobbling in front of the apparition. His mouth wobbled as well.

'W . . . w . . . w . . . w . . .' his mouth said.

'I think your team have just won,' said the apparition.

'W . . . w . . . w . . . w . . .' repeated Arthur, and punctuated each wobble with a prod at Ford Prefect's back. Ford was staring at the tumult in trepidation.

'You are English, aren't you?' said the apparition.

'W . . . w . . . w . . . w . . . yes,' said Arthur.

'Well, your team, as I say, have just won. The match. It means they retain the Ashes. You must be very pleased. I must say, I'm rather fond of cricket, though I wouldn't like anyone outside this planet to hear me saying that. Oh dear no.'

The apparition gave what looked as if it might have been a mischievous grin, but it was hard to tell because the sun was directly behind him, creating a blinding halo round his head and illuminating his silver hair and beard in a way which was awesome, dramatic and hard to reconcile with mischievous grins.

'Still,' he said, 'it'll all be over in a couple of days, won't it? Though as I said to you when we last met, I was very sorry about that. Still, whatever will have been, will have been.'

Arthur tried to speak, but gave up the unequal struggle. He prodded Ford again.

'I thought something terrible had happened,' said Ford, 'but it's just the end of the game. We ought to get out. Oh, hello, Slartibartfast, what are you doing here?'

'Oh, pottering, pottering,' said the old man gravely.

'That your ship? Can you give us a lift anywhere?'

'Patience, patience,' the old man admonished.

'OK,' said Ford. 'It's just that this planet's going to be demolished pretty soon.'

'I know that,' said Slartibartfast.

'And, well, I just wanted to make that point,' said Ford.

'The point is taken.'

'And if you feel that you really want to hang around a cricket pitch at this point . . .'

'I do.'

'Then it's your ship.'

'It is.'

'I suppose.' Ford turned away sharply at this point.

'Hello, Slartibartfast,' said Arthur at last.

'Hello, Earthman,' said Slartibartfast.

'After all,' said Ford, 'we can only die once.'

The old man ignored this and stared keenly on to the pitch, with eyes which seemed alive with expressions that had no apparent bearing on what was happening out there. What was happening was that the crowd was gathering itself into a wide circle round the centre of the pitch. What Slartibartfast saw in it, he alone knew.

Ford was humming something. It was just one note repeated at intervals. He was hoping that somebody would ask him what he was humming, but nobody did. If anybody had asked him he would have said he was humming the first line of a Noël Coward song called 'Mad About the Boy' over and over again. It would then have been pointed out to him that he was only singing one note, to which he would have replied that for reasons which he hoped would be apparent, he was omitting the 'about the boy' bit. He was annoyed that nobody asked.

'It's just,' he burst out at last, 'that if we don't go soon, we might get caught in the middle of it all again. And there's nothing that depresses me more than seeing a planet being destroyed. Except possibly still being on it when it happens. Or,' he added in an undertone, 'hanging around cricket matches.'

'Patience,' said Slartibartfast again. 'Great things are afoot.'

'That's what you said last time we met,' said Arthur.

'They were,' said Slartibartfast.

'Yes, that's true,' admitted Arthur.

All, however, that seemed to be afoot was a ceremony of some kind. It was being specially staged for the benefit of TV rather than the spectators, and all they could gather about it from where they were standing was what they heard from a nearby radio. Ford was aggressively uninterested.

He fretted as he heard it explained that the Ashes were about to be presented to the captain of the English team out there on the pitch, fumed when told that this was because they had now won them for the *n*th time, positively barked with annoyance at the information that the Ashes were the remains of a cricket stump, and when, further to this, he was asked to contend with the fact that the cricket stump in question had been burnt in Melbourne, Australia, in 1882, to signify the 'death of English cricket', he rounded on Slartibartfast, took a deep breath, but didn't have a chance to say anything because the old man wasn't there. He was marching out on to the pitch with terrible purpose in his gait, his hair, beard and robes swept behind him, looking very much as Moses would have looked if Sinai had been a well-cut lawn instead of, as it is more usually represented, a fiery smoking mountain.

'He said to meet him at his ship,' said Arthur.

'What in the name of Zarking fardwarks is the old fool doing?' exploded Ford.

'Meeting us at his ship in two minutes,' said Arthur with a shrug which indicated total abdication of thought. They started off towards it. Strange sounds reached their ears. They tried not to listen, but could not help noticing that Slartibartfast was querulously demanding that he be given the silver urn containing the Ashes, as they were, he said, 'vitally important for the past, present and safety of the Galaxy', and that this was causing wild hilarity. They resolved to ignore it.

What happened next they could not ignore. With a noise like a hundred thousand people saying 'wop', a steely white spaceship suddenly seemed to create itself out of nothing in the air directly above the cricket pitch and hung there with infinite menace and a slight hum.

Then for a while it did nothing, as if it expected everybody to go about their normal business and not mind it just hanging there.

Then it did something quite extraordinary. Or rather, it opened up and let something quite extraordinary come out of it, eleven quite extraordinary things.

They were robots, white robots.

What was most extraordinary about them was that they appeared to have come dressed for the occasion. Not only were they white, but they carried what appeared to be cricket bats, and not only that, but they also carried what appeared to be cricket balls, and not only that but they wore white ribbing pads round the lower parts of their legs. These last were extraordinary because they appeared to contain jets which allowed these curiously civilized robots to fly down from their hovering spaceship and start to kill people, which is what they did.

'Hello,' said Arthur, 'something seems to be happening.'

'Get to the ship,' shouted Ford. 'I don't want to know, just get to the ship.' He started to run. 'I don't want to know, I don't want to see, I don't want to hear,' he yelled as he ran, 'this is not my planet, I didn't choose to be here, I don't want to get involved, just get me out of here, and get me to a party, with people I can relate to!'

Smoke and flame billowed from the pitch.

'Well, the supernatural brigade certainly seems to be out in force here today . . .' burbled a radio happily to itself.

'What I need,' shouted Ford, by way of clarifying his previous remarks, 'is a strong drink and a peer-group.' He continued to run, pausing only for a moment to grab Arthur's arm and drag him along with him. Arthur had adopted his normal crisis role, which was to stand with his mouth hanging open and let it all wash over him.

'They're playing cricket,' muttered Arthur, stumbling along after Ford. 'I swear they are playing cricket. I do not know why they are doing this, but that is what they are doing. They're not just killing people, they're sending them up,' he shouted, 'Ford, they're sending us up!'

It would have been hard to disbelieve this without knowing a great deal more Galactic history than Arthur had so far managed to pick up in his travels. The ghostly but violent shapes that could be seen moving within the thick pall of smoke seemed to be performing a series of bizarre parodies of batting strokes, the difference being that every ball they struck with their bats exploded wherever it landed. The very first one of these had dispelled Arthur's initial reaction, that the whole thing might just be a publicity stunt by Australian margarine manufacturers.

And then, as suddenly as it had all started, it was over. The eleven white robots ascended through the seething cloud in a tight formation, and with a few last flashes of flame entered the bowels of their hovering white ship, which, with the noise of a hundred thousand people saying 'foop', promptly vanished into the thin air out of which it had wopped.

For a moment there was a terrible stunned silence, and then out of the drifting smoke emerged the pale figure of Slartibartfast looking even more like Moses because in spite of the continued absence of the mountain he was at least now striding across a fiery and smoking well-mown lawn.

He stared wildly about him until he saw the hurrying figures of Arthur Dent and Ford Prefect forcing their way through the frightened crowd which was for the moment busy stampeding in the opposite direction. The crowd was clearly thinking to itself about what an unusual day this was turning out to be, and not really knowing which way, if any, to turn.

Slartibartfast was gesticulating urgently at Ford and Arthur and shouting at them, as the three of them gradually converged on his ship, still parked behind the sight-screens and still apparently unnoticed by the crowd stampeding past it who presumably had enough of their own problems to cope with at that time.

'They've garble warble farble!' shouted Slartibartfast in his thin tremulous voice.

'What did he say?' panted Ford as he elbowed his way onwards.

Arthur shook his head.

'"They've . . ." something or other,' he said.

'They've table warble farble!' shouted Slartibartfast again.

Ford and Arthur shook their heads at each other.

'It sounds urgent,' said Arthur. He stopped and shouted.

'What?'

'They've garble warble fashes!' cried Slartibartfast, still waving at them.

'He says,' said Arthur, 'that they've taken the Ashes. That is what I think he says.' They ran on.

'The . . . ?' said Ford.

'Ashes,' said Arthur tersely. 'The burnt remains of a cricket stump. It's a trophy. That . . .' he was panting, 'is

. . . apparently . . . what they . . . have come and taken.' He shook his head very slightly as if he was trying to get his brain to settle down lower in his skull.

'Strange thing to want to tell us,' snapped Ford.

'Strange thing to take.'

'Strange ship.'

They had arrived at it. The second strangest thing about the ship was watching the Somebody Else's Problem field at work. They could now clearly see the ship for what it was simply because they knew it was there. It was quite apparent, however, that nobody else could. This wasn't because it was actually invisible or anything hyper-impossible like that. The technology involved in making anything invisible is so infinitely complex that nine hundred and ninety-nine thousand million, nine hundred and ninety-nine million, nine hundred and ninety-nine thousand, nine hundred and ninety-nine times out of a billion it is much simpler and more effective just to take the thing away and do without it. The ultra-famous sciento-magician Effrafax of Wug once bet his life that, given a year, he could render the great megamountain Magramal entirely invisible.

Having spent most of the year jiggling around with immense Lux-O-Valves and Refracto-Nullifiers and Spectrum-Bypass-O-Matics, he realized, with nine hours to go, that he wasn't going to make it.

So, he and his friends, and his friends' friends, and his friends' friends' friends, and his friends' friends' friends' friends, and some rather less good friends of theirs who happened to own a major stellar trucking company, put in what is now widely recognized as being the hardest night's work in history, and, sure enough, on the following day, Magramal was no longer visible. Effrafax lost his bet – and therefore his life – simply because some pedantic adjudicating official noticed (a) that when walking around the area that Magramal ought to be in he didn't trip over or break his nose on anything, and (b) a suspicious-looking extra moon.

The Somebody Else's Problem field is much simpler and effective, and what is more can be run for over a hundred years on a single torch battery. This is because it relies on people's natural predisposition not to see anything they don't want to, weren't expecting, or can't explain. If Effrafax had painted the mountain pink and erected a cheap and simple Somebody Else's Problem field on it, then people would have walked past the mountain, round it, even over it, and simply never have noticed that the thing was there.

And this is precisely what was happening with Slartibartfast's ship. It wasn't pink, but if it had been, that would have been the least of its visual problems and people were simply ignoring it like anything.

The most extraordinary thing about it was that it looked only partly like a spaceship with guidance fins, rocket engines and escape hatches and so on, and a great deal like a small upended Italian bistro.

Ford and Arthur gazed up at it with wonderment and deeply offended sensibilities.

'Yes, I know,' said Slartibartfast, hurrying up to them at that point, breathless and agitated, 'but there is a reason. Come, we must go. The ancient nightmare has come again. Doom confronts us all. We must leave at once.'

'I fancy somewhere sunny,' said Ford.

Ford and Arthur followed Slartibartfast into the ship and were so perplexed by what they saw inside it that they were totally unaware of what happened next outside.

A spaceship, yet another one, but this one sleek and

silver, descended from the sky on to the pitch, without fuss, its long legs unlocking in a smooth ballet of technology.

It landed gently. It extended a short ramp. A tall grey-green figure marched briskly out and approached the small knot of people who were gathered in the centre of the pitch tending to the casualties of the recent bizarre massacre. It moved people aside with quiet, understated authority, and came at last to a man lying in a desperate pool of blood, clearly now beyond the reach of any Earthly medicine, breathing, coughing his last. The figure knelt down quietly beside him.

'Arthur Philip Deodat?' asked the figure.

The man, with horrified confusion in eyes, nodded feebly.

'You're a no-good dumbo nothing,' whispered the creature. 'I thought you should know that before you went.'

5

Important facts from Galactic history, number two:
(Reproduced from the *Siderial Daily Mentioner's Book of Popular Galactic History*.)

Since this Galaxy began, vast civilizations have risen and fallen, risen and fallen, risen and fallen so often that it's quite tempting to think that life in the Galaxy must be

(a) something akin to seasick – space-sick, time sick, history sick or some such thing, and

(b) stupid.

6

It seemed to Arthur as if the whole sky suddenly just stood aside and let them through.

It seemed to him that the atoms of his brain and the atoms of the cosmos were streaming through each other.

It seemed to him that he was blown on the wind of the Universe, and that the wind was him.

It seemed to him that he was one of the thoughts of the Universe and that the Universe was a thought of his.

It seemed to the people at Lord's Cricket Ground that another North London restaurant had just come and gone as they so often do, and that this was Somebody Else's Problem.

'What happened?' whispered Arthur in considerable awe.

'We took off,' said Slartibartfast.

Arthur lay in startled stillness on the acceleration couch. He wasn't certain whether he had just got space-sickness or religion.

'Nice mover,' said Ford in an unsuccessful attempt to disguise the degree to which he had been impressed by what Slartibartfast's ship had just done, 'shame about the décor.'

For a moment or two the old man didn't reply. He was staring at the instruments with the air of one who is trying to convert Fahrenheit to centigrade in his head whilst his house is burning down. Then his brow cleared and he stared for a moment at the wide panoramic screen in front of him, which displayed a bewildering complexity of stars streaming like silver threads around them.

His lips moved as if he was trying to spell something. Suddenly his eyes darted in alarm back to his instruments, but then his expression merely subsided into a steady frown. He looked back up at the screen. He felt his own pulse. His frown deepened for a moment, then he relaxed.

'It's a mistake to try and understand machines,' he said, 'they only worry me. What did you say?'

'Décor,' said Ford. 'Pity about it.'

'Deep in the fundamental heart of mind and universe,' said Slartibartfast, 'there is a reason.'

Ford glanced sharply around. He clearly thought this was taking an optimistic view of things.

The interior of the flight deck was dark green, dark red, dark brown, cramped and moodily lit. Inexplicably, the resemblance to a small Italian bistro had failed to end at the hatchway. Small pools of light picked out pot plants, glazed tiles and all sorts of little unidentifiable brass things.

Raffia-wrapped bottles lurked hideously in the shadows.

The instruments which had occupied Slartibartfast's attention seemed to be mounted in the bottom of bottles which were set in concrete.

Ford reached out and touched it.

Fake concrete. Plastic. Fake bottles set in fake concrete.

The fundamental heart of mind and Universe can take a running jump, he thought to himself, this is rubbish. On the other hand, it could not be denied that the way the ship had moved made the *Heart of Gold* seem like an electric pram.

He swung himself off the couch. He brushed himself down. He looked at Arthur, who was singing quietly to himself. He looked at the screen and recognized nothing. He looked at Slartibartfast.

'How far did we just travel?' he said.

'About . . .' said Slartibartfast, 'about two-thirds of the way across the Galactic disc, I would say, roughly. Yes, roughly two-thirds, I think.'

'It's a strange thing,' said Arthur quietly, 'that the further and faster one travels across the Universe, the more one's position in it seems to be largely immaterial, and one is filled with a profound, or rather emptied of a . . .'

'Yes, very strange,' said Ford. 'Where are we going?'

'We are going,' said Slartibartfast, 'to confront an ancient nightmare of the Universe.'

'And where are you going to drop us off?'

'I will need your help.'

'Tough. Look, there's somewhere you can take us where we can have fun, I'm trying to think of it, we can get drunk and maybe listen to some extremely evil music. Hold on, I'll look it up.' He dug out his copy of *The Hitchhiker's Guide to the Galaxy* and zipped through those parts of the index primarily concerned with sex and drugs and rock and roll.

'A curse has arisen from the mists of time,' said Slartibartfast.

'Yes, I expect so,' said Ford. 'Hey,' he said, lighting accidentally on one particular reference entry, 'Eccentrica Gallumbits, did you ever meet her? The triple-breasted whore of Eroticon Six. Some people say her erogenous zones start some four miles from her actual body. Me, I disagree, I say five.'

'A curse,' said Slartibartfast, 'which will engulf the Galaxy in fire and destruction, and possibly bring the Universe to a premature doom. I mean it,' he added.

'Sounds like a bad time,' said Ford, 'with luck I'll be drunk enough not to notice. Here,' he said, stabbing his finger at the screen of the *Guide*, 'would be a really wicked place to go, and I think we should. What do you say, Arthur? Stop mumbling mantras and pay attention. There's important stuff you're missing here.'

Arthur pushed himself up from his couch and shook his head.

'Where are we going?' he said.

'To confront an ancient night—'

'Can it,' said Ford. 'Arthur, we are going out into the Galaxy to have some fun. Is that an idea you can cope with?'

'What's Slartibartfast looking so anxious about?' said Arthur.

'Nothing,' said Ford.

'Doom,' said Slartibartfast. 'Come,' he added, with sudden authority, 'there is much I must show and tell you.'

He walked towards a green wrought-iron spiral staircase set incomprehensibly in the middle of the flight deck and started to ascend. Arthur, with a frown, followed.

Ford slung the *Guide* sullenly back into his satchel.

'My doctor says that I have a malformed public-duty gland and a natural deficiency in moral fibre,' he muttered to himself, 'and that I am therefore excused from saving Universes.'

Nevertheless, he stomped up the stairs behind them.

What they found upstairs was just stupid, or so it seemed, and Ford shook his head, buried his face in his hands and slumped against a pot plant, crushing it against the wall.

'The central computational area,' said Slartibartfast unperturbed, 'this is where every calculation affecting the ship in any way is performed. Yes I know what it looks like, but it is in fact a complex four-dimensional topographical map of a series of highly complex mathematical functions.'

'It looks like a joke,' said Arthur.

'I know what it looks like,' said Slartibartfast, and went into it. As he did so, Arthur had a sudden vague flash of what it might mean, but he refused to believe it. The Universe could not possibly work like that, he thought, cannot possibly. That, he thought to himself, would be as absurd as, as absurd as . . . he terminated that line of thinking. Most of the really absurd things he could think of had already happened.

And this was one of them.

It was a large glass cage, or box – in fact a room.

In it was a table, a long one. Around it were gathered about a dozen chairs, of the bentwood style. On it was a tablecloth – a grubby, red and white check tablecloth, scarred with the occasional cigarette burn, each, presumably, at a precisely calculated mathematical position.

And on the tablecloth sat some dozen half-eaten Italian meals, hedged about with half-eaten breadsticks and half-drunk glasses of wine, and toyed with listlessly by robots.

It was all completely artificial. The robot customers were attended by a robot waiter, a robot wine waiter and a robot *maître d'*. The furniture was artificial, the tablecloth artificial, and each particular piece of food was clearly capable of exhibiting all the mechanical characteristics of, say, a *pollo sorpreso*, without actually being one.

And all participated in a little dance together – a complex routine involving the manipulation of menus, bill pads, wallets, cheque books, credit cards, watches, pencils and paper napkins, which seemed to be hovering constantly on the edge of violence, but never actually getting anywhere.

Slartibartfast hurried in, and then appeared to pass the time of day quite idly with the *maître d'*, whilst one of the customer robots, an autorory, slid slowly under the table, mentioning what he intended to do to some guy over some girl.

Slartibartfast took over the seat which had been thus vacated and passed a shrewd eye over the menu. The tempo of the routine round the table seemed somehow imperceptibly to quicken. Arguments broke out, people attempted to prove things on napkins. They waved fiercely at each other, and attempted to examine each other's pieces of chicken. The waiter's hand began to move on the bill pad more quickly than a human hand could manage, and then more quickly than a human eye could follow. The pace accelerated. Soon, an extraordinary and insistent politeness overwhelmed the group, and seconds later it seemed that a moment of consensus was suddenly achieved. A new vibration thrilled through the ship.

Slartibartfast emerged from the glass room.

'Bistromathics,' he said. 'The most powerful computational force known to parascience. Come to the Room of Informational Illusions.'

He swept past and carried them bewildered in his wake.

7

The Bistromathic Drive is a wonderful new method of crossing vast interstellar distances without all that dangerous mucking about with Improbability Factors.

Bistromathics itself is simply a revolutionary new way of understanding the behaviour of numbers. Just as Einstein observed that time was not an absolute but depended on the observer's movement in space, and that space was not an absolute, but depended on the observer's movement in time, so it is now realized that numbers are not absolute, but depend on the observer's movement in restaurants.

The first non-absolute number is the number of people for whom the table is reserved. This will vary during the course of the first three telephone calls to the restaurant, and then bear no apparent relation to the number of people who actually turn up, or to the number of people who subsequently join them after the show/match/party/gig, or to the number of people who leave when they see who else has turned up.

The second non-absolute number is the given time of arrival, which is now known to be one of those most bizarre of concepts, a recipriversexcluson, a number whose existence can only be defined as being anything other than itself. In other words, the given time of arrival is the one moment of time at which it is impossible that any member of the party will arrive. Recipriversexclusons now play a vital part in many branches of maths, including statistics and accountancy and also form the basic equations used to engineer the Somebody Else's Problem field.

The third and most mysterious piece of non-absoluteness of all lies in the relationship between the number of items on the bill, the cost of each item, the number of people at the table, and what they are each prepared to pay for. (The number of people who have actually brought any money is only a sub-phenomenon in this field.)

The baffling discrepancies which used to occur at this point remained uninvestigated for centuries simply because no one took them seriously. They were at the time put down to such things as politeness, rudeness, meanness, flashness, tiredness, emotionality, or the lateness of the hour, and completely forgotten about on the following morning. They were never tested under laboratory conditions, of course, because they never occurred in laboratories – not in reputable laboratories at least.

And so it was, only with the advent of pocket computers that the startling truth became finally apparent, and it was this:

Numbers written on restaurant bills within the confines of restaurants do not follow the same mathematical laws as numbers written on any other pieces of paper in any other parts of the Universe.

This single fact took the scientific world by storm. It completely revolutionized it. So many mathematical conferences got held in such good restaurants that many of the finest minds of a generation died of obesity and heart failure and the science of maths was put back by years.

Slowly, however, the implications of the idea began to be understood. To begin with it had been too stark, too crazy, too much what the man in the street would have said, 'Oh yes, I could have told you that,' about. Then some phrases like 'Interactive Subjectivity Frameworks' were invented, and everybody was able to relax and get on with it.

The small groups of monks who had taken up hanging around the major research institutes singing strange chants to the effect that the Universe was only a figment of its own imagination were eventually given a street theatre grant and went away.

8

'In space travel, you see,' said Slartibartfast, as he fiddled with some instruments in the Room of Informational Illusions, 'in space travel . . .'

He stopped and looked about him.

The Room of Informational Illusions was a welcome relief after the visual monstrosities of the central computational area. There was nothing in it. No information, no illusions, just themselves, white walls and a few small instruments which looked as if they were meant to plug into something which Slartibartfast couldn't find.

'Yes?' urged Arthur. He had picked up Slartibartfast's sense of urgency but didn't know what to do with it.

'Yes what?' said the old man.

'You were saying?'

Slartibartfast looked at him sharply.

'The numbers,' he said, 'are awful.' He resumed his search.

Arthur nodded wisely to himself. After a while he realized that this wasn't getting him anywhere and decided that he would say 'What?' after all.

'In space travel,' repeated Slartibartfast, 'all the numbers are awful.'

Arthur nodded again and looked round to Ford for help, but Ford was practising being sullen and getting quite good at it.

'I was only,' said Slartibartfast with a sigh, 'trying to save you the trouble of asking me why all the ship's computations were being done on a waiter's bill pad.'

Arthur frowned.

'Why,' he said, 'were all the ship's computations being done on a wait—'

He stopped.

Slartibartfast said, 'Because in space travel all the numbers are awful.'

He could tell that he wasn't getting his point across.

'Listen,' he said. 'On a waiter's bill pad numbers dance. You must have encountered the phenomenon.'

'Well . . .'

'On a waiter's bill pad,' said Slartibartfast, 'reality and unreality collide on such a fundamental level that each becomes the other and anything is possible, within certain parameters.'

'What parameters?'

'It's impossible to say,' said Slartibartfast. 'That's one of them. Strange but true. At least, I think it's strange,' he added, 'and I am assured that it's true.'

At that moment he located the slot in the wall for which he had been searching, and clicked the instrument he was holding into it.

'Do not be alarmed,' he said, and then suddenly darted an alarmed look at it himself, and lunged back, 'it's . . .'

They didn't hear what he said, because at that moment the ship winked out of existence around them and a star-battleship the size of a small Midlands industrial city plunged out of the sundered night towards them, star lasers ablaze.

A nightmare storm of blistering light seared through the blackness and smacked a fair bit off the planet directly behind them.

They gaped, pop-eyed, and were unable to scream.

9

Another world, another day, another dawn.

The early morning's thinnest sliver of light appeared silently.

Several billion trillion tons of superhot exploding hydrogen nuclei rose slowly above the horizon and managed to look small, cold and slightly damp.

There is a moment in every dawn when light floats, there is the possibility of magic. Creation holds its breath.

The moment passed as it regularly did on Sqornshellous Zeta, without incident.

The mist clung to the surface of the marshes. The swamp trees were grey with it, the tall reeds indistinct. It hung motionless like held breath.

Nothing moved.

There was silence.

The sun struggled feebly with the mist, tried to impart a little warmth here, shed a little light there, but clearly today was going to be just another long haul across the sky.

Nothing moved.

A long silence.

Nothing moved.

Silence.

Nothing moved.

Very often on Sqornshellous Zeta, whole days would go on like this, and this was indeed going to be one of them.

Fourteen hours later the sun sank hopelessly beneath the opposite horizon with a sense of totally wasted effort.

And a few hours later it reappeared, squared its shoulders and started on up the sky again.

This time, however, something was happening. A mattress had just met a robot.

'Hello, robot,' said the mattress.

'Bleah,' said the robot and continued what it was doing, which was walking round very slowly in a very tiny circle.

'Happy?' said the mattress.

The robot stopped and looked at the mattress. It looked at it quizzically. It was clearly a very stupid mattress. It looked back at him with wide eyes.

After what it had calculated to ten significant decimal places as being the precise length of pause most likely to convey a general contempt for all things mattressy, the robot continued to walk round in tight circles.

'We could have a conversation,' said the mattress, 'would you like that?'

It was a large mattress, and probably one of quite high quality. Very few things actually get manufactured these days, because in an infinitely large Universe such as, for instance, the one in which we live, most things one could possibly imagine, and a lot of things one would rather not, grow somewhere. A forest was discovered recently in which most of the trees grew ratchet screwdrivers as fruit. The life cycle of ratchet screwdriver fruit is quite interesting. Once picked it needs a dark dusty drawer in which it can lie undisturbed for years. Then one night it suddenly hatches, discards its outer skin which crumbles into dust, and emerges as a totally unidentifiable little metal object with flanges at both ends and a sort of ridge and a sort of a hole for a screw. This, when found, will get thrown away. No one knows what it is supposed to gain from this. Nature, in her infinite wisdom, is presumably working on it.

No one really knows what mattresses are meant to gain from their lives either. They are large, friendly, pocket-sprung creatures which live quiet private lives in the marshes of Sqornshellous Zeta. Many of them get caught, slaughtered, dried out, shipped out and slept on. None of them seem to mind this and all of them are called Zem.

'No,' said Marvin.

'My name,' said the mattress, 'is Zem. We could discuss the weather a little.'

Marvin paused again in his weary circular plod.

'The dew,' he observed, 'has clearly fallen with a particularly sickening thud this morning.'

He resumed his walk, as if inspired by this conversational outburst to fresh heights of gloom and despondency. He plodded tenaciously. If he had had teeth he would have gritted them at this point. He hadn't. He didn't. The mere plod said it all.

The mattress flolloped around. This is a thing that only live mattresses in swamps are able to do, which is why the word is not in more common usage. It flolloped in a sympathetic sort of way, moving a fairish body of water as it did so. It blew a few bubbles up through the water engagingly. Its blue and white stripes glistened briefly in a sudden feeble ray of sun that had unexpectedly made it through the mist, causing the creature to bask momentarily.

Marvin plodded.

'You have something on your mind, I think,' said the mattress, floopily.

'More than you can possibly imagine,' dreared Marvin. 'My capacity for mental activity of all kinds is as boundless as the infinite reaches of space itself. Except of course for my capacity for happiness.'

Stomp, stomp, he went.

'My capacity for happiness,' he added, 'you could fit into a matchbox without taking out the matches first.'

The mattress globbered. This is the noise made by a live, swamp-dwelling mattress that is deeply moved by a story of personal tragedy. The word can also, according to *The Ultra-Complete Maximegalon Dictionary of Every Language Ever*, mean the noise made by the Lord High Sanvalvwag of Hollop on discovering that he has forgotten his wife's birthday for the second year running. Since there was only ever one Lord High Sanvalvwag of Hollop, and he never married, the word is only ever used in a negative or speculative sense, and there is an ever-increasing body of opinion which holds that *The Ultra-Complete Maximegalon Dictionary* is not worth the fleet of lorries it takes to cart its microstored edition around in. Strangely enough, the dictionary omits the word 'floopily', which simply means 'in the manner of something which is floopy'.

The mattress globbered again.

'I sense a deep dejectedness in your diodes,' it vollued (for the meaning of the word 'vollue', buy a copy of *Squornshellous Swamp-talk* at any remaindered bookshop, or alternatively buy *The Ultra-Complete Maximegalon Dictionary*, as the University will be very glad to get it off their hands and regain some valuable parking lots), 'and it saddens me. You should be more mattresslike. We live quiet retired lives in the swamp, where we are content to flollop and vollue and regard the wetness in a fairly floopy manner. Some of us are killed, but all of us are called Zem so we never know which and globbering is thus kept to a minimum. Why are you walking in circles?'

'Because my leg is stuck,' said Marvin simply.

'It seems to me,' said the mattress eyeing it compassionately, 'that it is a pretty poor sort of leg.'

'You are right,' said Marvin, 'it is.'

'Voon,' said the mattress.

'I expect so,' said Marvin, 'and I also expect that you find the idea of a robot with an artificial leg pretty amusing. You should tell your friends Zem and Zem when you see them later, they'll laugh, if I know them, which I don't of course – except insofar as I know all organic life forms, which is much better than I would wish to. Ha, but my life is but a box of wormgears.'

He stomped around again in his tiny circle, around his thin steel peg-leg which revolved in the mud but seemed otherwise stuck.

'But why do you just keep walking round and round?' said the mattress.

'Just to make the point,' said Marvin, and continued, round and round.

'Consider it made, my dear friend,' flurbled the mattress, 'consider it made.'

'Just another million years,' said Marvin, 'just another quick million. Then I might try it backwards. Just for the variety, you understand.'

The mattress could feel deep in his innermost spring pockets that the robot dearly wished to be asked how long he had been trudging in this futile and fruitless manner, and with another quiet flurble he did so.

'Oh, just over the one-point-five-million mark, just over,' said Marvin airily. 'Ask me if I ever get bored, go on, ask me.'

The mattress did.

Marvin ignored the question, he merely trudged with added emphasis.

'I gave a speech once,' he said suddenly, and apparently unconnectedly. 'You may not instantly see why I bring the subject up, but that is because my mind works so phenomenally fast, and I am at a rough estimate thirty billion times more intelligent than you. Let me give you an example. Think of a number, any number.'

'Er, five,' said the mattress.

'Wrong,' said Marvin. 'You see?'

The mattress was much impressed by this and realized that it was in the presence of a not unremarkable mind. It willomied along its entire length, sending excited little ripples through its shallow algae-covered pool.

It gupped.

'Tell me,' it urged, 'of the speech you once made, I long to hear it.'

'It was received very badly,' said Marvin, 'for a variety of reasons. I delivered it,' he added, pausing to make an awkward humping sort of gesture with his not-exactly-good arm, but his arm which was better than the other one which was dishearteningly welded to his left side, 'over there, about a mile distance.'

He was pointing as well as he could manage, and he obviously wanted to make it totally clear that this was as well as he could manage, through the mist, over the reeds, to a part of the marsh which looked exactly the same as every other part of the marsh.

'There,' he repeated. 'I was somewhat of a celebrity at the time.'

Excitement gripped the mattress. It had never heard of speeches being delivered on Sqornshellous Zeta, and certainly not by celebrities. Water spattered off it as a thrill glurried across its back.

I did something which mattresses very rarely bother to do. Summoning every bit of its strength, it reared its oblong body, heaved it up into the air and held it quivering there for a few seconds whilst it peered through the mist over the reeds at the part of the marsh which Marvin had indicated, observing, without disappointment, that it was exactly the same as every other part of the marsh. The effort was too much, and it flodged back into its pool, deluging Marvin with smelly mud, moss and weeds.

'I was a celebrity,' droned the robot sadly, 'for a short while on account of my miraculous and bitterly resented escape from a fate almost as good as death in the heart of a blazing sun. You can guess from my condition,' he added, 'how narrow my escape was. I was rescued by a scrap-metal merchant, imagine that. Here I am, brain the size of . . . never mind.'

He trudged savagely for a few seconds.

'He it was who fixed me up with this leg. Hateful, isn't it? He sold me to a Mind Zoo. I was the star exhibit. I had to sit on a box and tell my story whilst people told me to cheer up and think positive. "Give us a grin, little robot," they would shout at me, "give us a little chuckle." I would explain to them that to get my face to grin would take a good couple of hours in a workshop with a wrench, and that went down very well.'

'The speech,' urged the mattress. 'I long to hear of the speech you gave in the marshes.'

'There was a bridge built across the marshes. A cyberstructured hyperbridge, hundreds of miles in length, to carry ion-buggies and freighters over the swamp.'

'A bridge?' quirruled the mattress. 'Here in the swamp?'

'A bridge,' confirmed Marvin, 'here in the swamp. It was going to revitalize the economy of the Sqornshellous system. They spent the entire economy of the

Sqornshellous system building it. They asked me to open it. Poor fools.'

It began to rain a little, a fine spray slid through the mist.

'I stood on the platform. For hundreds of miles in front of me, and hundreds of miles behind me, the bridge stretched.'

'Did it glitter?' enthused the mattress.

'It glittered.'

'Did it span the miles majestically?'

'It spanned the miles majestically.'

'Did it stretch like a silver thread far out into the invisible mist?'

'Yes,' said Marvin. 'Do you want to hear this story?'

'I want to hear your speech,' said the mattress.

'This is what I said. I said, "I would like to say that it is a very great pleasure, honour and privilege for me to open this bridge, but I can't because my lying circuits are all out of commission. I hate and despise you all. I now declare this hapless cyberstructure open to the unthinking abuse of all who wantonly cross her." And I plugged myself into the opening circuits.'

Marvin paused, remembering the moment.

The mattress flurred and glurried. It flolloped, gupped and willomied, doing this last in a particularly floopy way.

'Voon,' it wurfed at last. 'And was it a magnificent occasion?'

'Reasonably magnificent. The entire thousand-mile-long bridge spontaneously folded up its glittering spans and sank weeping into the mire, taking everybody with it.'

There was a sad and terrible pause at this point in the conversation during which a hundred thousand people seemed unexpectedly to say 'wop' and a team of white robots descended from the sky like dandelion seeds drifting on the wind in tight military formation. For a sudden violent moment they were all there, in the swamp, wrenching Marvin's false leg off, and then they were gone again in their ship, which said 'foop'.

'You see the sort of thing I have to contend with?' said Marvin to the gobbering mattress.

Suddenly, a moment later, the robots were back again for another violent incident, and this time when they left, the mattress was alone in the swamp. He flolloped around in astonishment and alarm. He almost lurgled in fear. He reared himself to see over the reeds, but there was nothing to see, no robot, no glittering bride, no ship, just more reeds. He listened, but there was no sound on the wind beyond the now familiar sound of half-crazed etymologists calling distantly to each other across the sullen mire.

10

The body of Arthur Dent span.

The Universe shattered into a million glittering fragments around it, and each particular shard span silently through the void, reflecting on its silver surface some single searing holocaust of fire and destruction.

And then the blackness behind the Universe exploded, and each particular piece of blackness was the furious smoke of hell.

And the nothingness behind the blackness behind the Universe erupted, and behind the nothingness behind the blackness behind the shattered Universe was at last the dark figure of an immense man speaking immense words.

'These, then,' said the figure, speaking from an immensely comfortable chair, 'were the Krikkit Wars, the greatest devastation ever visited upon our Galaxy. What you have experienced . . .'

Slartibartfast floated past, waving.

'It's just a documentary,' he called out. 'This is not a good bit. Terribly sorry, trying to find the rewind control . . .'

'. . . is what billions upon billions of innocent . . .'

'Do not,' called out Slartibartfast floating past again, and fiddling furiously with the thing that he had stuck into the wall of the Room of Informational Illusions and which was in fact still stuck there, 'agree to buy anything at this point.'

'. . . people, creatures, your fellow beings . . .'

Music swelled – again, it was immense music, immense chords. And behind the man, slowly, three tall pillars began to emerge out of the immensely swirling mist.

'. . . experienced, lived through – or, more often, failed to live through. Think of that, my friends. And let us not forget – and in just a moment I shall be able to suggest a way which will help us always to remember – that before the Krikkit Wars, the Galaxy was that rare and wonderful thing, a happy Galaxy!'

The music was going bananas with immensity at this point.

'A happy Galaxy, my friends, as represented by the symbol of the Wikkit Gate!'

The three pillars stood out clearly now, three pillars topped with two cross pieces in a way which looked stupefyingly familiar to Arthur's addled brain.

'The three pillars,' thundered the man. 'The Steel Pillar which represented the Strength and Power of the Galaxy!'

Searchlights seared out and danced crazy dances up and down the pillar on the left which was, clearly, made of steel or something very like it. The music thumped and bellowed.

'The Perspex Pillar,' announced the man, 'representing the forces of Science and Reason in the Galaxy!'

Other searchlights played exotically up and down the right-hand, transparent pillar creating dazzling patterns within it and a sudden inexplicable craving for ice-cream in the stomach of Arthur Dent.

'And,' the thunderous voice continued, 'the Wooden Pillar, representing . . .' and here his voice became just very slightly hoarse with wonderful sentiments, 'the forces of Nature and Spirituality.'

The lights picked out the central pillar. The music moved bravely up into the realms of complete unspeakability.

'Between them supporting,' the voice rolled on, approaching its climax, 'the Golden Bail of Prosperity and the Silver Bail of Peace!'

The whole structure was now flooded with dazzling lights, and the music had now, fortunately, gone far beyond the limits of the discernible. At the top of the three pillars the two brilliantly gleaming bails sat and dazzled. There seemed to be girls sitting on top of them, or maybe they were meant to be angels. Angels are usually represented as wearing more than that, though.

Suddenly there was a dramatic hush in what was presumably meant to be the Cosmos, and a darkening of the lights.

'There is not a world,' thrilled the man's expert voice,

'not a civilized world in the Galaxy where this symbol is not revered even today. Even in primitive worlds it persists in racial memories. This it was that the forces of Krikkit destroyed, and this it is that now locks their world away till the end of eternity!'

And with a flourish, the man produced in his hands a model of the Wikkit Gate. Scale was terribly hard to judge in this whole extraordinary spectacle, but the model looked as if it must have been about three feet high.

'Not the original key, of course. That, as everyone knows, was destroyed, blasted into the ever-whirling eddies of the space–time continuum and lost for ever. This is a remarkable replica, hand-tooled by skilled craftsmen, lovingly assembled using ancient craft secrets into a memento you will be proud to own, in memory of those who fell, and in tribute to the Galaxy – our Galaxy – which they died to defend . . .'

Slartibartfast floated past again at this moment.

'Found it,' he said. 'We can lose all this rubbish. Just don't nod, that's all.'

'Now, let us bow our heads in payment,' intoned the voice, and then said it again, much faster and backwards.

Lights came and went, the pillars disappeared, the man gabbled himself backwards into nothing, the Universe snappily reassembled itself around them.

'You get the gist?' said Slartibartfast.

'I'm astonished!' said Arthur, 'and bewildered.'

'I was asleep,' said Ford, who floated into view at this point. 'Did I miss anything?'

They found themselves once again teetering rather rapidly on the edge of an agonizingly high cliff. The wind whipped out from their faces and across a bay on which the remains of one of the greatest and most powerful space battle-fleets ever assembled in the Galaxy was briskly burning itself back into existence. The sky was a sullen pink, darkening via a rather curious colour to blue and upwards to black. Smoke billowed down out of it at an incredible lick.

Events were now passing back by them almost too quickly to be distinguished, and when, a short while later, a huge star-battleship rushed away from them as if they'd said 'boo', they only just recognized it as the point at which they had come in.

But now things were too rapid, a video-tactile-blur which brushed and jiggled them through centuries of Galactic history, turning, twisting, flickering. The sound was a mere thin thrill.

Periodically throughout the thickening jumble of events they sensed appalling catastrophes, deep horrors, cataclysmic shocks, and these were always associated with certain recurring images, the only images which ever stood out clearly from the avalanche of tumbling history: a wicket gate, a small hard red ball, hard white robots, and also something less distinct, something dark and cloudy.

But there was also another sensation which rose clearly out of the trilling passage of time.

Just as a slow series of clicks when speeded up will lose the definition of each individual click and gradually take on the quality of a sustained and rising tone, so a series of individual impressions here took on the quality of a sustained emotion – and yet not an emotion. If it was an emotion, it was a totally emotionless one. It was hatred, implacable hatred. It was cold, not like ice is cold, but like a wall is cold. It was impersonal, not like a randomly flung fist in a crowd is impersonal, but like a computer-issued parking summons is impersonal. And it was deadly – again, not like a bullet or a knife is deadly, but like a brick wall across a motorway is deadly.

And just as a rising tone will change in character and take on harmonics as it rises, so again, this emotionless emotion seemed to rise to an unbearable if unheard scream and suddenly seemed to be a scream of guilt and failure.

And suddenly it stopped.

They were left standing on a quiet hilltop on a tranquil evening.

The sun was setting.

All around them softly undulating green countryside rolled off gently into the distance. Birds sang about what they thought of it all, and the general opinion seemed to be good. A little way away could be heard the sound of children playing, and a little further away than the apparent source of that sound could be seen in the dimming evening light the outlines of a small town.

The town appeared to consist mostly of fairly low buildings made of white stone. The skyline was of gentle pleasing curves.

The sun had nearly set.

As if out of nowhere, music began. Slartibartfast tugged at a switch and it stopped.

A voice said, 'This . . .' Slartibartfast tugged at a switch and it stopped.

'I will tell you about it,' he said quietly.

The place was peaceful. Arthur felt happy. Even Ford seemed cheerful. They walked a short way in the direction of the town, and the Informational Illusion of the grass was pleasant and springy under their feet, and the Informational Illusion of the flowers smelt sweet and fragrant. Only Slartibartfast seemed apprehensive and out of sorts.

He stopped and looked up.

It suddenly occurred to Arthur that, coming as this did at the end, so to speak, or rather the beginning of all the horror they had just blurrily experienced, something nasty must be about to happen. He was distressed to think that something nasty could happen to somewhere as idyllic as this. He too glanced up. There was nothing in the sky.

'They're not about to attack here, are they?' he said. He realized that this was merely a recording he was walking through, but he still felt alarmed.

'Nothing is about to attack here,' said Slartibartfast in a voice which unexpectedly trembled with emotion. 'This is where it all starts. This is the place itself. This is Krikkit.'

He stared up into the sky.

The sky, from one horizon to another, from east to west, from north to south, was utterly and completely black.

11

Stomp stomp.

Whirrr.

'Pleased to be of service.'

'Shut up.'

'Thank you.'

Stomp stomp stomp stomp stomp.

Whirrr.

'Thank you for making a simple door very happy.'

'Hope your diodes rot.'

'Thank you. Have a nice day.'

Stomp stomp stomp stomp.

Whirrr.

'It is my pleasure to open for you . . .'

'Zark off.'

'. . . and my satisfaction to close again with the knowledge of a job well done.'

'I said Zark off.'

'Thank you for listening to this message.'

Stomp stomp stomp stomp.

'Wop.'

Zaphod stopped stomping. He had been stomping around the *Heart of Gold* for days, and so far no door had said 'wop' to him. He was fairly certain that no door had said 'wop' to him now. It was not the sort of thing doors said. Too concise. Furthermore, there were not enough doors. It sounded as if a hundred thousand people had said 'wop', which puzzled him because he was the only person on the ship.

It was dark. Most of the ship's non-essential systems were closed down. It was drifting idly in a remote area of the Galaxy, deep in the inky blackness of space. So which particular hundred thousand people would turn up at this point and say a totally unexpected 'wop'?

He looked about him, up the corridor and down the corridor. It was all in deep shadow. There were just the very dim pinkish outlines to the doors which glowed in the dark and pulsed whenever they spoke, though he had tried every way he could think of of stopping them.

The lights were off so that his heads could avoid looking at each other, because neither of them was currently a particularly engaging sight, and nor had they been since he had made the error of looking into his soul.

It had indeed been an error.

It had been late one night – of course.

It had been a difficult day – of course.

There had been soulful music playing on the ship's sound system – of course.

And he had, of course, been slightly drunk.

In other words, all the usual conditions which bring on a bout of soul-searching had applied, but it had, nevertheless, clearly been an error.

Standing now, silent and alone, in the dark corridor he remembered the moment and shivered. His one head looked one way and his other the other and each decided that the other was the way to go.

He listened but could hear nothing.

All there had been was the 'wop'.

It seemed an awfully long way to bring an awfully large number of people just to say one word.

He started nervously to edge his way in the direction of the bridge. There at least he would feel in control. He stopped again. The way he was feeling he didn't think he was an awfully good person to be in control.

The first shock of that moment, thinking back, had been discovering that he actually had a soul.

In fact he'd always more or less assumed that he had one as he had a full complement of everything else, and indeed two of somethings, but suddenly actually to encounter the thing lurking there deep within him had given him a severe jolt.

And then to discover (this was the second shock) that it wasn't the totally wonderful object which he felt a man in his position had a natural right to expect had jolted him again.

Then he had thought about what his position actually was and the renewed shock had nearly made him spill his drink. He drained it quickly before anything serious happened to it. He then had another quick one to follow the first one down and check that it was all right.

'Freedom,' he said aloud.

Trillian came on to the bridge at that point and said several enthusiastic things on the subject of freedom.

'I can't cope with it,' he said darkly, and sent a third drink down to see why the second hadn't yet reported on the condition of the first. He looked uncertainly at both of her and preferred the one on the right.

He poured a drink down his other throat with the plan that it would head the previous one off at the pass, join forces with it, and together they would get the second to pull itself together. Then all three would go off in search of the fuss, give it a good talking to and maybe a bit of a sing as well.

He felt uncertain as to whether the fourth drink had understood all that, so he sent down a fifth to explain the plan more fully and a sixth for moral support.

'You're drinking too much,' said Trillian.

His heads collided trying to sort out the four of her he could now see into a whole person. He gave up and looked at the navigation screen and was astonished to see a quite phenomenal number of stars.

'Excitement and adventure and really wild things,' he muttered.

'Look,' she said in a sympathetic tone of voice, and sat down near him, 'it's quite understandable that you're going to feel a little aimless for a bit.'

He boggled at her. He had never seen anyone sit on their own lap before.

'Wow,' he said. He had another drink.

'You've finished the mission you've been on for years.'

'I haven't been on it. I've tried to avoid being on it.'

'You've still finished it.'

He grunted. There seemed to be a terrific party going on in his stomach.

'I think it finished me,' he said. 'Here I am, Zaphod Beeblebrox, I can go anywhere, do anything. I have the greatest ship in the known sky, a girl with whom things seem to be working out pretty well . . .'

'Are they?'

'As far as I can tell. I'm not an expert in personal relationships . . .'

Trillian raised her eyebrows.

'I am,' he added, 'one hell of a guy, I can do anything I want only I just don't have the faintest idea what.'

He paused.

'One thing,' he further added, 'has suddenly ceased to lead to another' – in contradiction of which he had another drink and slid gracelessly off his chair.

Whilst he slept it off, Trillian did a little research in the ship's copy of *The Hitchhiker's Guide to the Galaxy*. It had some advice to offer on drunkenness.

'Go to it,' it said, 'and good luck.'

It was cross-referenced to the entry concerning the size of the Universe and ways of coping with that.

Then she found the entry on Han Wavel, an exotic holiday planet, and one of the wonders of the Galaxy.

Han Wavel is a world which consists largely of fabulous ultra-luxury hotels and casinos, all of which have been formed by the natural erosion of wind and rain.

The chances of this happening are more or less one to infinity against. Little is known of how this came about because none of the geophysicists, probability statisticians, meteoranalysts or bizzarrologists who are so keen to research it can afford to stay there.

Terrific, thought Trillian to herself, and within a few hours the great white running-shoe ship was slowly powering down out of the sky beneath a hot brilliant sun towards a brightly coloured sandy spaceport The ship was clearly causing a sensation on the ground, and Trillian was enjoying herself. She heard Zaphod moving around and whistling somewhere in the ship.

'How are you?' she said over the general intercom.

'Fine,' he said brightly, 'terribly well.'

'Where are you?'

'In the bathroom.'

'What are you doing?'

'Staying here.'

After an hour or two it became plain that he meant it and the ship returned to the sky without having once opened its hatchway.

'Heigh ho,' said Eddie the computer.

Trillian nodded patiently, tapped her fingers a couple of times and pushed the intercom switch.

'I think that enforced fun is probably not what you need at this point.'

'Probably not,' replied Zaphod from wherever he was.

'I think a bit of physical challenge would help draw you out of yourself.'

'Whatever you think, I think,' said Zaphod.

'RECREATIONAL IMPOSSIBILITIES' was a heading which caught Trillian's eye when, a short while later, she sat down to flip through the *Guide* again, and as the *Heart of Gold* rushed at improbable speeds in an indeterminate direction, she sipped a cup of something undrinkable from the Nutrimatic drinks dispenser and read about how to fly.

The Hitchhiker's Guide to the Galaxy has this to say on the subject of flying.

There is an art, it says, or rather, a knack to flying.

The knack lies in learning how to throw yourself at the ground and miss.

Pick a nice day, it suggests, and try it.

The first part is easy.

All it requires is simply the ability to throw yourself forward with all your weight, and the willingness not to mind that it's going to hurt.

That is, it's going to hurt if you fail to miss the ground.

Most people fail to miss the ground, and if they are really trying properly, the likelihood is that they will fail to miss it fairly hard.

Clearly, it is this second part, the missing, which presents the difficulties.

One problem is that you have to miss the ground accidentally. It's no good deliberately intending to miss the ground because you won't. You have to have your attention suddenly distracted by something else when you're halfway there, so that you are no longer thinking about falling, or about the ground, or about how much it's going to hurt if you fail to miss it.

It is notoriously difficult to prise your attention away from these three things during the split second you have at your disposal. Hence most people's failure, and their eventual disillusionment with this exhilarating and spectacular sport.

If, however, you are lucky enough to have your attention momentarily distracted at the crucial moment by, say, a gorgeous pair of legs (tentacles, pseudopodia, according to phylum and/or personal inclination) or a bomb going off in your vicinity, or by suddenly spotting an extremely rare species of beetle crawling along a nearby twig, then in your astonishment you will miss the ground completely and remain bobbing just a few inches above it in what might seem to be a slightly foolish manner.

This is a moment for superb and delicate concentration.

Bob and float, float and bob.

Ignore all considerations of your own weight and simply let yourself waft higher.

Do not listen to what anybody says to you at this point because they are unlikely to say anything helpful.

They are most likely to say something along the lines of, 'Good God, you can't possibly be flying!'

It is vitally important not to believe them or they will suddenly be right.

Waft higher and higher.

Try a few swoops, gentle ones at first, then drift above the treetops breathing regularly.

DO NOT WAVE AT ANYBODY.

When you have done this a few times you will find the moment of distraction rapidly becomes easier and easier to achieve.

You will then learn all sorts of things about how to control your flight, your speed, your manoeuvrability, and the trick usually lies in not thinking too hard about whatever you want to do, but just – allowing it to happen as if it was going to anyway.

You will also learn about how to land properly, which is something you will almost certainly cock up, and cock up badly, on your first attempt.

There are private flying clubs you can join which help you achieve the all-important moment of distraction. They hire people with surprising bodies or opinions to leap out from behind bushes and exhibit and/or explain them at the critical moments. Few genuine hitchhikers will be able to afford to join these clubs, but some may be able to get temporary employment at them.

Trillian read this longingly, but reluctantly decided that Zaphod wasn't really in the right frame of mind for attempting to fly, or for walking through mountains or for trying to get the Brantisvogan Civil Service to acknowledge a change-of address card, which were the other things listed under the heading 'Recreational Impossibilities'.

Instead, she flew the ship to Allosimanius Syneca, a world of ice, snow, mind-hurtling beauty and stunning cold. The trek from the snow plains of Liska to the summit of the Ice Crystal Pyramids of Sastantua is long and gruelling, even with jet skis and a team of Syneca Snowhounds, but the view from the top, a view which takes in the stin Glacier Fields, the shimmering Prism Mountains and the far ethereal dancing icelights, is one which first freezes the mind and then slowly releases it to hitherto unexperienced horizons of beauty, and Trillian, for one, felt that she could do with a bit of having her mind slowly released to hitherto unexperienced horizons of beauty.

They went into a low orbit.

There lay the silverwhite beauty of Allosimanius Syneca beneath them.

Zaphod stayed in bed with one head stuck under a pillow and the other doing crosswords till late into the night.

Trillian nodded patiently again, counted to a sufficiently high number, and told herself that the important thing now was just to get Zaphod talking.

She prepared, by dint of deactivating all the robot kitchen synthomatics, the most fabulously delicious meal she could contrive – delicately oiled meats, scented fruits, fragrant cheeses, fine Aldebaran wines.

She carried it through to him and asked if he felt like talking things through.

'Zark off,' said Zaphod.

Trillian nodded patiently to herself, counted to an even higher number, tossed the tray lightly aside, walked to the transport room and just teleported herself the hell out of his life.

She didn't even programme any coordinates, she hadn't the faintest idea where she was going, she just went – a random row of dots flowing through the Universe.

'Anything,' she said to herself as she left, 'is better than this.'

'Good job too,' muttered Zaphod to himself, turned over and failed to go to sleep.

The next day he restlessly paced the empty corridors of the ship, pretending not to look for her, though he knew she wasn't there. He ignored the computer's querulous demands to know just what the hell was going on around here by fitting a small electronic gag across a pair of its terminals.

After a while he began to turn down the lights. There was nothing to see. Nothing was about to happen.

Lying in bed one night – and night was now virtually continuous on the ship – he decided to pull himself together, to get things into some of perspective. He sat up sharply and started to pull clothes on. He decided that there must be someone in the Universe feeling more wretched, miserable and forsaken than himself, and he determined to set out and find him.

Halfway to the bridge it occurred to him that it might be Marvin, and he returned to bed.

It was a few hours later than this, as he stomped disconsolately about the darkened corridors swearing at cheerful doors, that he heard the 'wop' said, and it made him very nervous.

He leant tensely against the corridor wall and frowned like a man trying to unbend a corkscrew by telekinesis. He laid his fingertips against the wall and felt an unusual vibration. And now he could quite clearly hear slight noises, and could hear where they were coming from – they were coming from the bridge.

Moving his hand along the wall he came across something he was glad to find. He moved on a little further, quietly.

'Computer?' he hissed.

'Mmmm?' said the computer terminal nearest him, equally quietly.

'Is there someone on this ship?'

'Mmmmm,' said the computer.

'Who is it?'

'Mmmmm mmm mmmmm,' said the computer.

'What?'

'Mmmmm mmmm mm mmmmmmmm.'

Zaphod buried one of his faces in two of his hands.

'Oh, Zarquon,' he muttered to himself. Then he stared up the corridor towards the entrance to the bridge in the dim distance from which more and purposeful noises were coming, and in which the gagged terminals were situated.

'Computer,' he hissed again.

'Mmmmm?'

'When I ungag you . . .'

'Mmmmm.'

'Remind me to punch myself in the mouth.'

'Mmmmm mmm?'

'Either one. Now just tell me this. One for yes, two for no. Is it dangerous?'

'Mmmm.'

'It is?'

'Mmmm.'

'You didn't just go "mmmm" twice?'

'Mmmm mmmm.'

'Hmmmm.'

He inched his way up the corridor as if he would rather be yarding his way down it, which was true.

He was within two yards of the door to the bridge when he suddenly realized to his horror that it was going to be nice to him, and he stopped dead. He hadn't been able to turn off the doors' courtesy voice circuits.

This doorway to the bridge was concealed from view within it because of the excitingly chunky way in which the bridge had been designed to curve round, and he had been hoping to enter unobserved.

He leant despondently back against the wall again and said some words which his other head was quite shocked to hear.

He peered at the dim pink outline of the door, and discovered that in the darkness of the corridor he could just about make out the sensor field which extended out into the corridor and told the door when there was someone there for whom it must open and to whom it must make a cheery and pleasant remark.

He pressed himself hard back against the wall and edged himself towards the door, flattening his chest as much as he possibly could to avoid brushing against the very, very dim perimeter of the field. He held his breath, and congratulated himself on having lain in bed sulking for the last few days rather than trying to work out his feelings on chest expanders in the ship's gym.

He then realized he was going to have to speak at this point.

He took a series of very shallow breaths, and then said as quickly and as quietly as he could, 'Door, if you can hear me, say so very very quietly.'

Very very quietly, the door murmured, 'I can hear you.'

'Good. Now, in a moment, I'm going to ask you to

open. When you open I do not want you to say that you enjoyed it, OK?'

'OK.'

'And I don't want you to say to me that I have made a simple door very happy, or that it is your pleasure to open for me and your satisfaction to close again with the knowledge of a job well done, OK?'

'OK.'

'And I do not want you to ask me to have a nice day, understand?'

'I understand.'

'OK,' said Zaphod, tensing himself, 'open now.'

The door slid open quietly. Zaphod slipped quietly through. The door closed quietly behind him.

'Is that the way you like it, Mr Beeblebrox?' said the door out loud.

'I want you to imagine,' said Zaphod to the group of white robots who swung round to stare at him at that point, 'that I have an extremely powerful Kill-O-Zap blaster pistol in my hand.'

There was an immensely cold and savage silence. The robots regarded him with hideously dead eyes. They stood very still. There was something intensely macabre about their appearance, especially to Zaphod who had never seen one before or ever known anything about them. The Krikkit Wars belonged to the ancient past of the Galaxy, and Zaphod had spent most of his early history lessons plotting how he was going to have sex with the girl in the cybercubicle next to him, and since his teaching computer had been an integral part of this plot it had eventually had all its history circuits wiped and replaced with an entirely different set of ideas which had then resulted in it being scrapped and sent to a home for Degenerate Cybermats, whither it was followed by the girl who had inadvertently fallen deeply in love with the unfortunate machine, with the result (a) that Zaphod never got near her and (b) that he missed out on a period of ancient history that would have been of inestimable value to him at this moment.

He stared at them in shock.

It was impossible to explain why, but their smooth and sleek white bodies seemed to be the utter embodiment of clean, clinical evil. From their hideously dead eyes to their powerful lifeless feet, they were clearly the calculated product of a mind that wanted simply to kill. Zaphod gulped in cold fear.

They had been dismantling part of the rear bridge wall, and had forced a passage through some of the vital innards of the ship. Through the tangled wreckage Zaphod could see, with a further and worse sense of shock, that they were tunnelling towards the very heart of the ship, the heart of the Improbability Drive that had been so mysteriously created out of thin air, the *Heart of Gold* itself.

The robot closest to him was regarding him in such a way as to suggest that it was measuring every smallest particle of his body, mind and capability. And when it spoke, what it said seemed to bear this impression out. Before going on to what it actually said, it is worth recording at this point that Zaphod was the first living organic being to hear one of these creatures speak for something over ten billion years. If he had paid more attention to his ancient history lessons and less to his organic being, he might have been more impressed by this honour.

The robot's voice was like its body, cold, sleek and lifeless. It had almost a cultured rasp to it. It sounded as ancient as it was.

It said, 'You do have a Kill-O-Zap blaster pistol in your hand.'

Zaphod didn't know what it meant for a moment, but then he glanced down at his own hand and was relieved to see that what he had found clipped to a wall bracket was indeed what he had thought it was.

'Yeah,' he said in a kind of relieved sneer, which is quite tricky, 'well, I wouldn't want to overtax your imagination, robot.' For a while nobody said anything, and Zaphod realized that the robots were obviously not here to make conversation, and that it was up to him.

'I can't help noticing that you have parked your ship,' he said with a nod of one of his heads in the appropriate direction, 'through mine.'

There was no denying this. Without regard for any kind of proper dimensional behaviour they had simply materialized their ship precisely where they wanted it to be, which meant that it was simply locked through the *Heart of Gold* as if they were nothing more than two combs.

Again, they made no response to this, and Zaphod wondered if the conversation would gather any momentum if he phrased his part of it in the form of questions.

'. . . haven't you?' he added.

'Yes,' replied the robot.

'Er, OK,' said Zaphod. 'So what are you cats doing here?'

Silence.

'Robots,' said Zaphod, 'what are you robots doing here?'

'We have come,' rasped the robot, 'for the Gold Bail.'

Zaphod nodded. He waggled his gun to invite further elaboration. The robot seemed to understand this.

'The Gold Bail is part of the Key we seek,' continued the robot, 'to release our Masters from Krikkit.'

Zaphod nodded again. He waggled his gun again.

'The Key,' continued the robot simply, 'was disintegrated in time and space. The Golden Bail is embedded in the device which drives your ship. It will be reconstituted in the Key. Our Masters shall be released. The Universal Readjustment will continue.'

Zaphod nodded again.

'What are you talking about?' he said.

A slightly pained expression seemed to cross the robot's totally expressionless face. He seemed to be finding the conversation depressing.

'Obliteration,' it said. 'We seek the Key,' it repeated, 'we already have the Wooden Pillar, the Steel Pillar and the Perspex Pillar. In a moment we will have the Gold Bail . . .'

'No you won't.'

'We will,' stated the robot.

'No you won't. It makes my ship work.'

'In a moment,' repeated the robot patiently, 'we will have the Gold Bail . . .'

'You will not,' said Zaphod.

'And then we must go,' said the robot, in all seriousness, 'to a party.'

'Oh,' said Zaphod, startled. 'Can I come?'

'No,' said the robot. 'We are going to shoot you.'

'Oh yeah?' said Zaphod, waggling his gun.

'Yes,' said the robot, and they shot him.

Zaphod was so surprised that they had to shoot him again before he fell down.

12

'Shhh,' said Slartibartfast. 'Listen and watch.'

Night had now fallen on ancient Krikkit. The sky was

dark and empty. The only light was coming from the nearby town, from which pleasant convivial sounds were drifting quietly on the breeze. They stood beneath a tree from which heady fragrances wafted around them. Arthur squatted and felt the Informational Illusion of the soil and the grass. He ran it through his fingers. The soil seemed heavy and rich, the grass strong. It was hard to avoid the impression that this was a thoroughly delightful place in all respects.

The sky was, however, extremely blank and seemed to Arthur to cast a certain chill over the otherwise idyllic, if currently invisible, landscape. Still, he supposed, it's a question of what you're used to.

He felt a tap on his shoulder and looked up. Slartibartfast was quietly directing his attention to something down the other side of the hill. He looked and could just see some faint lights dancing and waving, and moving slowly in their direction.

As they came nearer, sounds became audible too, and soon the dim lights and noises resolved themselves into a small group of people who were walking home across the hill towards the town.

They walked quite near the watchers beneath the tree, swinging lanterns which made soft and crazy lights dance among the trees and grass, chattering contentedly, and actually singing a song about how terribly nice everything was, how happy they were, how much they enjoyed working on the farm, and how pleasant it was to be going home to see their wives and children, with a lilting chorus to the effect that the flowers were smelling particularly nice at this time of year and that it was a pity the dog had died seeing as it liked them so much. Arthur could almost imagine Paul McCartney sitting with his feet up by the fire one evening, humming it to Linda and wondering what to buy with the proceeds, and thinking probably Essex.

'The Masters of Krikkit,' breathed Slartibartfast in sepulchral tones.

Coming, as it did, so hard upon the heels of his own thoughts about Essex this remark caused Arthur a moment's confusion. Then the logic of the situation imposed itself on his scattered mind, and he discovered that he still didn't understand what the old man meant.

'What?' he said.

'The Masters of Krikkit,' said Slartibartfast again, and if his breathing had been sepulchral before, this time he sounded like someone in Hades with bronchitis.

Arthur peered at the group and tried to make sense of what little information he had at his disposal at this point.

The people in the group were clearly alien, if only because they seemed a little tall, thin, angular and almost as pale as to be white, but otherwise they appeared remarkably pleasant; a little whimsical perhaps, one wouldn't necessarily want to spend a long coach journey with them, but the point was that if they deviated in any way from being good straightforward people it was in being perhaps too nice rather than not nice enough. So why all this rasping lungwork from Slartibartfast which would seem more appropriate to a radio commercial for one of those nasty films about chainsaw operators taking their work home with them?

Then, this Krikkit angle was a tough one, too. He hadn't quite fathomed the connection between what he knew as cricket, and what . . .

Slartibartfast interrupted his train of thought at this point as if sensing what was going through his mind.

'The game you know as cricket,' he said, and his voice

still seemed to be wandering lost in subterranean passages, 'is just one of those curious freaks of racial memory which can keep images alive in the mind aeons after their true significance has been lost in the mists of time. Of all the races in the Galaxy, only the English could possibly revive the memory of the most horrific wars ever to sunder the Universe and transform it into what I'm afraid is generally regarded as an incomprehensibly dull and pointless game.

'Rather fond of it myself,' he added, 'but in most people's eyes you have been inadvertently guilty of the most grotesquely bad taste. Particularly the bit about the little red ball hitting the wicket, that's very nasty.'

'Um,' said Arthur with a reflective frown to indicate that his cognitive synapses were coping with this as best they could, 'um.'

'And these,' said Slartibartfast, slipping back into crypt guttural and indicating the group of Krikkit men who had now walked past them, 'are the ones who started it all, and it will start tonight. Come, we will follow, and see why.'

They slipped out from underneath the tree, and followed the cheery party along the dark hill path. Their natural instinct was to tread quietly and stealthily in pursuit of their quarry, though, as they were simply walking through a recorded Informational Illusion, they could as easily have been wearing euphoniums and woad for all the notice their quarry would have taken of them.

Arthur noticed that a couple of members of the party were now singing a different song. It came lilting back to them through the soft night air, and was a sweet romantic ballad which would have netted McCartney Kent and Sussex and enabled him to put in a fair offer for Hampshire.

'You must surely know,' said Slartibartfast to Ford, 'what it is that is about to happen?'

'Me?' said Ford. 'No.'

'Did you not learn ancient galactic history when you were a child?'

'I was in the cybercubicle behind Zaphod,' said Ford, 'it was very distracting. Which isn't to say that I didn't learn some pretty stunning things.'

At this point Arthur noticed a curious feature to the song that the party were singing. The middle eight bridge, which would have had McCartney firmly consolidated in Winchester and gazing intently over the Test Valley to the rich pickings of the New Forest beyond, had some curious lyrics. The songwriter was referring to meeting with a girl not 'under the moon' or 'beneath the stars' but 'above the grass', which struck Arthur as being a little prosaic. Then he looked up again at the bewilderingly blank sky, and had the distinct feeling that there was an important point here, if only he could grasp what it was. It gave him a feeling of being alone in the Universe, and he said so.

'No,' said Slartibartfast, with a slight quickening of his step, 'the people of Krikkit have never thought to themselves "We are alone in the Universe." They are surrounded by a huge dust cloud, you see, their single sun with its single world, and they are right out on the utmost eastern edge of the Galaxy. Because of the dust cloud there has never been anything to see in the sky. At night it is totally blank. During the day there is the sun, but you can't look directly at that so they don't. They are hardly aware of the sky. It's as if they had a blind spot which extended 180 degrees from horizon to horizon.

'You see, the reason why they have never thought

"We are alone in the Universe" is that until tonight they don't know about the Universe. Until tonight.'

He moved on, leaving the words ringing in the air behind him.

'Imagine,' he said, 'never even thinking "We are alone" simply because it has never occurred to you to think that there's any other way to be.'

He moved on again.

'I'm afraid this is going to be a little unnerving,' he added.

As he spoke, they became aware of a very thin roaring scream high up in the sightless sky above them. They glanced upwards in alarm, but for a moment or two could see nothing.

Then Arthur noticed that the people in the party in front of them had heard the noise, but that none of them seemed to know what to do with it. They were glancing around themselves in consternation, left, right, forwards, backwards, even at the ground. It never occurred to them to look upwards.

The profoundness of the shock and horror they emanated a few moments later when the burning wreckage of a spaceship came hurtling and screaming out of the sky and crashed about half a mile from where they were standing was something that you had to be there to experience.

Some speak of the *Heart of Gold* in hushed tones, some of the *Starship Bistromath*.

Many speak of the legendary and gigantic *Starship Titanic*, a majestic and luxurious cruise-liner launched from the great shipbuilding asteroid complexes of Artrifactovol some hundreds of years ago now, and with good reason.

It was sensationally beautiful, staggeringly huge, and

more pleasantly equipped than any ship in what now remains of history (see note below on the Campaign for Real Time) but it had the misfortune to be built in the very earliest days of Improbability Physics, long before this difficult and cussed branch of knowledge was fully, or at all, understood.

The designers and engineers decided, in their innocence, to build a prototype Improbability Field into it, which was meant, supposedly, to ensure that it was Infinitely Improbable that anything would ever go wrong with any part of the ship.

They did not realize that because of the quasi-reciprocal and circular nature of all Improbability calculations, anything that was Infinitely Improbable was actually very likely to happen almost immediately.

The *Starship Titanic* was a monstrously pretty sight as it lay beached like a silver Arcturan Megavoidwhale amongst the laser-lit tracery of its construction gantries, a brilliant cloud of pins and needles of light against the deep interstellar blackness; but when launched, it did not even manage to complete its very first radio message – an SOS – before undergoing a sudden and gratuitous total existence failure.

However, the same event which saw the disastrous failure of one science in its infancy also witnessed the apotheosis of another. It was conclusively proved that more people watched tri-D TV coverage of the launch than actually existed at the time, and this has now been recognized as the greatest achievement ever in the science of audience research.

Another spectacular media event of that time was the supernova which the star Ysllodins underwent a few hours later. Ysllodins is the star around which most of the Galaxy's major insurance underwriters live, or rather lived.

But whilst these spaceships, and other great ones which come to mind, such as the Galactic Fleet Battleships – the GSS *Daring*, the GSS *Audacity* and the GSS *Suicidal Insanity* – are all spoken of with awe, pride, enthusiasm, affection, admiration, regret, jealousy, resentment, in fact most of the better-known emotions, the one which regularly commands the most actual astonishment was *Krikkit One*, the first spaceship ever built by the people of Krikkit.

This is not because it was a wonderful ship. It wasn't.

It was crazy piece of near junk. It looked as if it had been knocked up in somebody's backyard, and this was in fact precisely where it had been knocked up. The astonishing thing about the ship was not that it was done well (it wasn't) but that it was done at all. The period of time which had elapsed between the moment that the people of Krikkit had discovered that there was such a thing as space and the launching of this their first spaceship was almost exactly a year.

Ford Prefect was extremely grateful as he strapped himself in, that this was just another Informational Illusion, and that he was therefore completely safe. In real life it wasn't a ship he would have set foot in for all the rice wine in China. 'Extremely rickety' was one phrase which sprang to mind, and 'Please may I get out?' was another.

'This is going to fly?' said Arthur, giving gaunt looks at the lashed-together pipework and wiring which festooned the cramped interior of the ship.

Slartibartfast assured him that it would, that they were perfectly safe and that it was all going to be extremely instructive and not a little harrowing.

Ford and Arthur decided just to relax and be harrowed.

'Why not,' said Ford, 'go mad?'

In front of them and, of course, totally unaware of their presence for the very good reason that they weren't actually there, were the three pilots. They also had constructed the ship. They had been on the hill path that night singing wholesome heartwarming songs. Their brains had been very slightly turned by the nearby crash of the alien spaceship. They had spent weeks stripping every tiniest last secret out of the wreckage of that burnt-up spaceship, all the while singing lilting spaceship-stripping ditties. They had then built their own ship and this was it. This was their ship, and they were currently singing a little song about that too, expressing the twin joys of achievement and ownership. The chorus was a little poignant, and told of their sorrow that their work had kept them such long hours in the garage, away from the company of their wives and children, who had missed them terribly but had kept them cheerful by bringing them continual stories of how nicely the puppy was growing up.

Pow, they took off.

They roared into the sky like a ship that knew precisely what it was doing.

'No way,' said Ford a while later after they had recovered from the shock of acceleration, and were climbing up out of the planet's atmosphere, 'no way,' he repeated, 'does anyone design and build a ship like this in a year, no matter how motivated. I don't believe it. Prove it to me and I still won't believe it.' He shook his head thoughtfully and gazed out of a tiny port at the nothingness outside it.

The trip passed uneventfully for a while, and Slartibartfast fast-wound them through it.

Very quickly, therefore, they arrived at the inner

perimeter of the hollow, spherical dust cloud which surrounded their sun and home planet, occupying, as it were, the next orbit out.

It was more as if there was a gradual change in the texture and consistency of space. The darkness seemed now to thrum and ripple past them. It was a very cold darkness, a very blank and heavy darkness, it was the darkness of the night sky of Krikkit.

The coldness and heaviness and blankness of it took a slow grip on Arthur's heart, and he felt acutely aware of the feelings of the Krikkit pilots which hung in the air like a thick static charge. They were now on the very boundary of the historical consciousness of their race. This was the very limit beyond which none of them had ever speculated, or even known that there was any speculation to be done.

The darkness of the cloud buffeted at the ship. Inside was the silence of history. Their historic mission was to find out if there was anything or anywhere on the other side of the sky, from which the wrecked spaceship could have come, another world maybe, strange and incomprehensible though this thought was to the enclosed minds of those who had lived beneath the sky of Krikkit.

History was gathering itself to deliver another blow.

Still the darkness thrummed at them, the blank enclosing darkness. It seemed closer and closer, thicker and thicker, heavier and heavier. And suddenly it was gone.

They flew out of the cloud.

They saw the staggering jewels of the night in their infinite dust and their minds sang with fear.

For a while they flew on, motionless against the starry sweep of the Galaxy, itself motionless against the infinite sweep of the Universe. And then they turned round.

'It'll have to go,' the men of Krikkit said as they headed back for home.

On the way back they sang a number of tuneful and reflective songs on the subjects of peace, justice, morality, culture, sport, family life and the obliteration of all other life forms.

13

'So you see,' said Slartibartfast, slowly stirring his artificially constructed coffee, and thereby also stirring the whirlpool interfaces between real and unreal numbers, between the interactive perceptions of mind and Universe, and thus generating the restructured matrices of implicitly enfolded subjectivity which allowed his ship to reshape the very concept of time and space, 'how it is.'

'Yes,' said Arthur.

'Yes,' said Ford.

'What do I do,' said Arthur, 'with this piece of chicken?'

Slartibartfast glanced at him gravely.

'Toy with it,' he said, 'toy with it.'

He demonstrated with his own piece.

Arthur did so, and felt the slight tingle of a mathematical function thrilling through the chicken leg as it moved four-dimensionally through what Slartibartfast had assured him was five-dimensional space.

'Overnight,' said Slartibartfast, 'the whole population of Krikkit was transformed from being charming, delightful, intelligent . . .'

'. . . if whimsical . . .' interpolated Arthur.

'. . . ordinary people,' said Slartibartfast, 'into charming, delightful, intelligent . . .'

'. . . whimsical . . .'

'. . . manic xenophobes. The idea of a Universe didn't fit into their world picture, so to speak. They simply couldn't cope with it. And so, charmingly, delightfully, intelligently, whimsically if you like, they decided to destroy it. What's the matter now?'

'I don't like this wine very much,' said Arthur sniffing it.

'Well, send it back. It's all part of the mathematics of it.'

Arthur did so. He didn't like the topography of the waiter's smile, but he'd never liked graphs anyway.

'Where are we going?' said Ford.

'Back to the Room of Informational Illusions,' said Slartibartfast, rising and patting his mouth with the mathematical representation of a paper napkin, 'for the second half.'

14

'The people of Krikkit,' said His High Judgmental Supremacy, Judiciary Pag, LIVR (the Learned, Impartial and Very Relaxed), Chairman of the Board of Judges at the Krikkit War Crimes Trial, 'are, well, you know, they're just a bunch of real sweet guys, you know, who just happen to want to kill everybody. Hell, I feel the same way some mornings. Shit.

'OK,' he continued, swinging his feet up on to the bench in front of him and pausing a moment to pick a thread off his Ceremonial Beach Loafers, 'so you wouldn't necessarily want to share a Galaxy with these guys.'

This was true.

The Krikkit attack on the Galaxy had been stunning. Thousands and thousands of huge Krikkit warships had leapt suddenly out of hyperspace and simultaneously attacked thousands and thousands of major worlds, first seizing vital material supplies for building the next wave, and then calmly zapping those worlds out of existence.

The Galaxy, which had been enjoying a period of unusual peace and prosperity at the time, reeled like a man getting mugged in a meadow.

'I mean,' continued Judiciary Pag, gazing round the ultra-modern (this was ten billion years ago, when 'ultra-modern' meant lots of stainless steel and brushed concrete) and huge courtroom, 'these guys are just *obsessed.*'

This too was true, and is the only explanation anyone has yet managed to come up with for the unimaginable speed with which the people of Krikkit had pursued their new and absolute purpose – the destruction of everything that wasn't Krikkit.

It is also the only explanation for their bewilderingly sudden grasp of all the hypertechnology involved in building their thousands of spaceships, and their millions of lethal white robots.

These had really struck terror into the hearts of everyone who had encountered them – in most cases, however, the terror was extremely short-lived, as was the person experiencing the terror. They were savage, single-minded flying battle machines. They wielded formidable multifunctional battleclubs which, brandished one way, would knock down buildings and, brandished another way, fired blistering Omni-Destruct-O-Zap rays and, brandished a third way, launched a hideous arsenal of grenades, ranging from minor incendiary devices to Maxi-Slorta Hypernuclear Devices which could take out a major sun. Simply striking the grenades with the battleclubs simultaneously primed them and launched them with phenomenal accuracy over distances ranging from mere yards to hundreds of thousands of miles.

'OK,' said Judiciary Pag again, 'so we won.' He paused and chewed a little gum. 'We won,' he repeated, 'but that's no big deal. I mean a medium-sized galaxy against one little world, and how long did it take us? Clerk of the Court?'

'M'lud?' said the severe little man in black, rising.

'How long, kiddo?'

'It is a trifle difficult, m'lud, to be precise in this matter. Time and distance . . .'

'Relax, guy, be vague.'

'I hardly like to be vague, m'lud, over such a . . .'

'Bite the bullet and be it.'

The Clerk of the Court blinked at him. It was clear that like most of the Galactic legal profession he found Judiciary Pag (or Zipo Bibrok 5×10^8, as his private name was known, inexplicably, to be) a rather distressing figure. He was clearly a bounder and a cad. He seemed to think that the fact that he was the possessor of the finest legal mind ever discovered gave him the right to behave exactly as he liked, and unfortunately he appeared to be right.

'Er, well, m'lud, very approximately, two thousand years,' the Clerk murmured unhappily.

'And how many guys zilched out?'

'Two grillion, m'lud.' The Clerk sat down. A hydrospectic photo of him at this point would have revealed that he was steaming slightly.

Judiciary Pag gazed once more around the courtroom, wherein were assembled hundreds of the very highest officials of the entire Galactic administration, all in their ceremonial uniforms or bodies, depending on metabolism and custom. Behind a wall of Zap-Proof Crystal stood a representative group of the people of Krikkit, looking with calm, polite loathing at all the aliens gathered to pass judgment on them. This was the most momentous occasion in legal history, and Judiciary Pag knew it.

He took out his chewing gum and stuck it under his chair.

'That's a whole lotta stiffs,' he said quietly.

The grim silence in the courtroom seemed in accord with this view.

'So, like I said, these are a bunch of really sweet guys, but you wouldn't want to share a Galaxy with them, not if they're just gonna keep at it, not if they're not gonna learn to relax a little. I mean it's just gonna be continual nervous time, isn't it, right? Pow, pow, pow, when are they next coming at us? Peaceful coexistence is just right out, right? Get me some water somebody, thank you.'

He sat back and sipped reflectively.

'OK,' he said, 'hear me, hear me. It's, like, these guys, you know, are entitled to their own view of the Universe. And according to their view, which the Universe forced on them, right, they did right. Sounds crazy, but I think you'll agree. They believe in . . .'

He consulted a piece of paper which he found in the back pocket of his Judicial jeans.

'They believe in "peace, justice, morality, culture, sport, family life and the obliteration of all other life forms".'

He shrugged.

'I've heard a lot worse,' he said.

He scratched his crotch reflectively.

'Freeeow,' he said. He took another sip of water, then held it up to the light and frowned at it. He twisted it round.

'Hey, is there something in this water?' he said.

'Er, no, m'lud,' said the Court Usher who had brought it to him, rather nervously.

'Then take it away,' snapped Judiciary Pag, 'and put something in it. I got an idea.'

He pushed away the glass and leaned forward.

'Hear me, hear me,' he said.

The solution was brilliant, and went like this:

The planet of Krikkit was to be encased for perpetuity in an envelope of Slo-Time, inside which life would continue almost infinitely slowly. All light would be deflected round the envelope so that it would remain invisible and impenetrable. Escape from the envelope would be utterly impossible unless it were unlocked from the outside.

When the rest of the Universe came to its final end, when the whole of creation reached its dying fall (this was all, of course, in the days before it was known that the end of the Universe would be a spectacular catering venture) and life and matter ceased to exist, then the planet of Krikkit and its sun would emerge from its Slo-Time envelope and continue a solitary existence, such as it craved, in the twilight of the Universal void.

The Lock would be on an asteroid which would slowly orbit the envelope.

The Key would be the symbol of the Galaxy – the Wikkit Gate.

By the time the applause in the court had died down, Judiciary Pag was already in the Sens-O-Shower with a rather nice member of the jury that he'd slipped a note to half an hour earlier.

15

Two months later, Zipo Bibrok 5×10^8 had cut the bottoms off his galactic state jeans, and was spending part of the enormous fee his judgments commanded lying on a jewelled beach having Essence of Qualactin rubbed into his back by the same rather nice member of the jury. She was a Soolfinian girl from beyond the Cloudworlds of Yaga. She had skin like lemon silk and was very interested in legal bodies.

'Did you hear the news?' she said.

'Weeeelaaaaah!' said Zipo Bibrok 5×10^8, and you would have had to have been there to know exactly why he said this. None of this was on the tape of Informational Illusions, and is all based on hearsay.

'No,' he added, when the thing that had made him say 'Weeeeelaaaaah' had stopped happening. He moved his body round slightly to catch the first rays of the third and greatest of primeval Vod's three suns which was now creeping over the ludicrously beautiful horizon, and the sky now glittered with some of the greatest tanning power ever known.

A fragrant breeze wandered up from the quiet sea, trailed along the beach, and drifted back to sea again, wondering where to go next. On a mad impulse it went up to the beach again. It drifted back to sea.

'I hope it isn't good news,' muttered Zipo Bibrok 5×10^8, ''cos I don't think I could bear it.'

'Your Krikkit judgment was carried out today,' said the girl sumptuously. There was no need to say such a straightforward thing sumptuously, but she went ahead and did it anyway because it was that sort of day. 'I heard it on the radio,' she said, 'when I went back to the ship for the oil.'

'Uhuh,' murmured Zipo and rested his head back on the jewelled sand.

'Something happened,' she said.

'Mmmm?'

'Just after the Slo-Time envelope was locked,' she said, and paused a moment from rubbing in the Essence of Qualactin, 'a Krikkit warship which had been missing presumed destroyed turned out to be just missing after all. It appeared and tried to seize the Key.'

Zipo sat up sharply.

'Hey, what?' he said.

'It's all right,' she said in a voice which would have calmed the Big Bang down. 'Apparently there was a short battle. The Key and the warship were disintegrated and blasted into the space–time continuum. Apparently they are lost for ever.'

She smiled, and ran a little more Essence of Qualactin on to her fingertips. He relaxed and lay back down.

'Do what you did a moment or two ago,' he murmured.

'That?' she said.

'No, no,' he said, 'that.'

She tried again.

'That? she asked.

'Weeeeelaaaaaah!'

Again, you had to be there.

The fragrant breeze drifted up from the sea again.

A magician wandered along the beach, but no one needed him.

16

'Nothing is lost for ever,' said Slartibartfast, his face flickering redly in the light of the candle which the robot waiter was trying to take away, 'except for the Cathedral of Chalesm.'

'The what?' said Arthur with a start.

'The Cathedral of Chalesm,' repeated Slartibartfast. 'It was during the course of my researches at the Campaign for Real Time that I—'

'The what?' said Arthur again.

The old man paused and gathered his thoughts, for what he hoped would be one last onslaught on this story. The robot waiter moved through the space–time matrices in a way which spectacularly combined the surly with the obsequious, made a snatch for the candle and got it. They had had the bill, had argued convincingly about who had had the cannelloni and how many bottles of wine they had had, and, as Arthur had been dimly aware, had thereby successfully manoeuvred the ship out of subjective space and into parking orbit round a strange planet. The waiter was now anxious to complete his part of the charade and clear the bistro.

'All will become clear,' said Slartibartfast.

'When?'

'In a minute. Listen. The time streams are now very polluted. There's a lot of muck floating about in them, flotsam and jetsam, and more and more of it is now being regurgitated into the physical world. Eddies in the space–time continuum, you see.'

'So I hear,' said Arthur.

'Look, where are we going?' said Ford, pushing his chair back from the table with impatience. 'Because I'm eager to get there.'

'We are going,' said Slartibartfast, in a slow, measured voice, 'to try to prevent the war robots of Krikkit from regaining the whole of the Key they need to unlock the planet of Krikkit from the Slo-Time envelope and release the rest of their army and their mad Masters.'

'It's just,' said Ford, 'that you mentioned a party.'

'I did,' said Slartibartfast, and hung his head.

He realized that it had been a mistake, because the idea seemed to exercise a strange and unhealthy fascination on the mind of Ford Prefect. The more that Slartibartfast unravelled the dark and tragic story of Krikkit and its people, the more Ford Prefect wanted to drink a lot and dance with girls.

The old man felt that he should not have mentioned the party until he absolutely had to. But there it was, the fact was out, and Ford Prefect had attached himself to it the way an Arcturan Megaleach attaches itself to its victim before biting his head off and making off with his spaceship.

'When,' said Ford eagerly, 'do we get there?'

'When I've finished telling you why we have to go there.'

'I know why I'm going,' said Ford, and leaned back, sticking his hands behind his head. He gave one of his smiles which made people twitch.

Slartibartfast had hoped for an easy retirement.

He had been planning to learn to play the octaventral heebie-phone – a pleasantly futile task, he knew, because he had the wrong number of mouths.

He had also been planning to write an eccentric and relentlessly inaccurate monograph on the subject of equatorial fjords in order to set the record wrong about one or two matters he saw as important.

Instead, he had somehow got talked into doing some part-time work for the Campaign for Real Time and had started to take it all seriously for the first time in his life. As a result he now found himself spending his fast-declining years combating evil and trying to save the Galaxy.

He found it exhausting work and sighed heavily.

'Listen,' he said, 'at Camtim—'

'What?' said Arthur.

'The Campaign for Real Time, which I will tell you about later. I noticed that five pieces of jetsam which had in relatively recent times plopped back into existence seemed to correspond to the five pieces of the missing Key. Only two I could trace exactly – the Wooden Pillar, which appeared on your planet, and the Silver Bail. It seems to be at some sort of party. We must go there to retrieve it before the Krikkit robots find it, or who knows what may happen?'

'No,' said Ford firmly. 'We must go to the party in order to drink a lot and dance with girls.'

'But haven't you understood everything I . . . ?'

'Yes,' said Ford, with a sudden and unexpected fierceness, 'I've understood it all perfectly well. That's why I want to have as many drinks and dance with as many girls as possible while there are still any left. If everything you've shown us is true . . .'

'True? Of course it's true.'

'. . . then we don't stand a whelk's chance in a supernova.'

'A what?' said Arthur sharply again. He had been following the conversation doggedly up to this point, and was keen not to lose the thread now.

'A whelk's chance in a supernova,' repeated Ford without losing momentum. 'The—'

'What's a whelk got to do with a supernova?' said Arthur.

'It doesn't,' said Ford levelly, 'stand a chance in one.'

He paused to see if the matter was now cleared up. The freshly puzzled looks clambering across Arthur's face told him that it wasn't.

'A supernova,' said Ford as quickly and as clearly as he could, 'is a star which explodes at almost half the speed of light and burns with the brightness of a billion suns and then collapses as a super-heavy neutron star. It's a star which burns up other stars, got it? Nothing stands a chance in a supernova.'

'I see,' said Arthur.

'The—'

'So why a whelk particularly?'

'Why not a whelk? Doesn't matter.'

Arthur accepted this, and Ford continued, picking up his early fierce momentum as best he could.

'The point is,' he said, 'that people like you and me, Slartibartfast, and Arthur – particularly and especially Arthur – are just dilletantes, eccentrics, layabouts, fartarounds if you like.'

Slartibartfast frowned, partly in puzzlement and partly in umbrage. He started to speak.

'– . . .' is as far as he got.

'We're not obsessed by anything, you see,' insisted Ford.

'. . .'

'And that's the deciding factor. We can't win against obsession. They care, we don't. They win.'

'I care about lots of things,' said Slartibartfast, his voice trembling partly with annoyance, but partly also with uncertainty.

'Such as?'

'Well,' said the old man, 'life, the Universe. Everything, really. Fjords.'

'Would you die for them?'

'Fjords?' blinked Slartibartfast in surprise. 'No.'

'Well, then.'

'Wouldn't see the point, to be honest.'

'And I still can't see the connection,' said Arthur, 'with whelks.'

Ford could feel the conversation slipping out of his control, and refused to be sidetracked by anything at this point.

'The point is,' he hissed, 'that we are not obsessive people, and we don't stand a chance against . . .'

'Except for your sudden obsession with whelks,' pursued Arthur, 'which I still haven't understood.'

'Will you please leave whelks out of it?'

'I will if you will,' said Arthur. 'You brought the subject up.'

'It was an error,' said Ford, 'forget them. The point is this.'

He leant forward and rested his forehead on the tips of his fingers.

'What was I talking about?' he said wearily.

'Let's just go down to the party,' said Slartibartfast, 'for whatever reason.' He stood up, shaking his head.

'I think that's what I was trying to say,' said Ford.

For some unexplained reason, the teleport cubicles were in the bathroom.

17

Time travel is increasingly regarded as a menace. History is being polluted.

The Encyclopaedia Galactica has much to say on the theory and practice of time travel, most of which is incomprehensible to anyone who hasn't spent at least four lifetimes studying advanced hypermathematics, and since it was impossible to do this before time travel was invented, there is a certain amount of confusion as to how the idea was arrived at in the first place. One rationalization of this problem states that time travel was, by its very nature, discovered simultaneously at all periods of history, but this is clearly bunk.

The trouble is that a lot of history is now quite clearly bunk as well.

Here is an example. It may not seem to be an important one to some people, but to others it is crucial. It is certainly significant in that it was this single event which caused the Campaign for Real Time to be set up in the first place (or is it last? It depends which way round you see history as happening, and this too is now an increasingly vexed question).

There is, or was, a poet. His name was Lallafa, and he wrote what are widely regarded throughout the Galaxy as being the finest poems in existence, the *Songs of the Long Land*.

They are/were unspeakably wonderful. That is to say, you couldn't speak very much of them at once without being so overcome with emotion, truth and a sense of the wholeness and oneness of things that you wouldn't pretty soon need a brisk walk round the block, possibly pausing at a bar on the way back for a quick glass of perspective and soda. They were that good.

Lallafa had lived in the forests of the Long Lands of Effa. He lived there, and he wrote his poems there. He wrote them on pages made of dried habra leaves, without the benefit of education or correcting fluid. He wrote about the light in the forest and what he thought about that. He wrote about the darkness in the forest, and what he thought about that. He wrote about the girl who had left him and precisely what he thought about that.

Long after his death his poems were found and wondered over. News of them spread like morning sunlight. For centuries they illuminated and watered the lives of many people whose lives might otherwise have been darker and drier.

Then, shortly after the invention of time travel, some major correcting fluid manufacturers wondered whether his poems might have been better still if he had had access to some high-quality correcting fluid, and whether he might be persuaded to say a few words to that effect.

They travelled the time waves, they found him, they explained the situation – with some difficulty – to him, and did indeed persuade him. In fact they persuaded him to such effect that he became extremely rich at their hands, and the girl about whom he was otherwise destined to write with such precision never got around to leaving him, and in fact they moved out of the forest to a rather nice pad in town and he frequently commuted to the future to do chat shows, on which he sparkled wittily.

He never got around to writing the poems, of course, which was a problem, but an easily solved one. The manufacturers of correcting fluid simply packed him off for a week somewhere with a copy of a later edition of his book and a stack of dried habra leaves to copy them out on to, making the odd deliberate mistake and correction on the way.

Many people now say that the poems are suddenly worthless. Others argue that they are exactly the same as they always were, so what's changed? The first people say that that isn't the point. They aren't quite certain what the point is, but they are quite sure that that isn't it. They set up the Campaign for Real Time to try to stop this sort of thing going on. Their case was considerably strengthened by the fact that a week after they had set themselves up, news broke that not only had the great Cathedral of Chalesm been pulled down in order to build a new ion refinery, but that the construction of the refinery had taken so long, and had had to extend so far back into the past in order to allow ion production to start on time, that the Cathedral of Chalesm had now never been built in the first place. Picture postcards of the cathedral suddenly became immensely valuable.

So a lot of history is now gone for ever. The Campaign for Real Timers claim that just as easy travel eroded the differences between one country and another, and between one world and another, so time travel is now eroding the differences between one age and another. 'The past,' they say, 'is now truly like a foreign country. They do things exactly the same there.'

18

Arthur materialized, and did so with all the customary staggering about and clasping at his throat, heart and various limbs which he still indulged himself in whenever he made any of these hateful and painful materializations that he was determined not to let himself get used to.

He looked around for the others.

They weren't there.

He looked around for the others again.

They still weren't there.

He closed his eyes.

He opened them.

He looked around for the others.

They obstinately persisted in their absence.

He closed his eyes again, preparatory to making this completely futile exercise once more, and because it was only then, whilst his eyes were closed, that his brain began to register what his eyes had been looking at whilst they were open, a puzzled frown crept across his face.

So he opened his eyes again to check his facts and the frown stayed put.

If anything, it intensified, and got a good firm grip. If this was a party it was a very bad one, so bad, in fact, that everyone else had left. He abandoned this line of thought as futile. Obviously this wasn't a party. It was a cave, or a labyrinth, or a tunnel or something – there was insufficient light to tell. All was darkness, a damp shiny darkness. The only sounds were the echoes of his own breathing, which sounded worried. He coughed very slightly, and then had to listen to the thin ghostly echo of his cough trailing away amongst winding corridors and sightless chambers, as of some great labyrinth, and eventually returning to him via the same unseen corridors, as if to say . . . 'Yes?'

This happened to every slightest noise he made, and it unnerved him. He tried to hum a cheery tune, but by the time it returned to him it was a hollow dirge and he stopped.

His mind was suddenly full of images from the story that Slartibartfast had been telling him. He half-expected suddenly to see lethal white robots step silently from the shadows and kill him. He caught his breath. They didn't. He let it go again. He didn't know what he did expect.

Someone or something, however, seemed to be expecting him, for at that moment there lit up suddenly in the dark distance an eerie green neon sign.

It said, silently:

YOU HAVE BEEN DIVERTED

The sign flicked off again, in a way which Arthur was not at all certain he liked. It flicked off with a sort of contemptuous flourish. Arthur then tried to assure himself that this was just a ridiculous trick of his imagination. A neon sign is either on or off, depending on whether it has electricity running through it or not. There was no way, he told himself, that it could possibly effect the transition from one state to the other with a contemptuous flourish. He hugged himself tightly in his dressing gown and shivered, nevertheless.

The neon sign in the depths now suddenly lit up, bafflingly, with just three dots and a comma. Like this:

. . . ,

Only in green neon.

It was trying, Arthur realized after staring at this perplexedly for a second or two, to indicate that there was more to come, that the sentence was not complete. Trying with almost superhuman pedantry, he further reflected. Or at least, inhuman pedantry.

The sentence then completed itself with these two words:

ARTHUR DENT.

He reeled. He steadied himself to have another clear look at it. It still said ARTHUR DENT, so he reeled again.

Once again, the sign flicked off, and left him blinking in the darkness with just the dim red image of his name jumping on his retina.

WELCOME, the sign now suddenly said.

After a moment, it added:

I DON'T THINK.

The stone cold fear which had been hovering around Arthur all this time, waiting for its moment, recognized that its moment had now come and pounced on him. He tried to fight it off. He dropped into a kind of alert crouch that he had once seen somebody do on television, but it must have been someone with stronger knees. He peered huntedly into the darkness.

'Er, hello?' he said.

He cleared his throat and said it again, more loudly and without the 'er'. At some distance down the corridor it seemed suddenly as if somebody started to beat on a bass drum.

He listened to it for a few seconds and realized that it was just his heart beating.

He listened for a few seconds more and realized that it wasn't his heart, it was somebody down the corridor beating on a bass drum.

Beads of sweat formed on his brow, tensed themselves, and leapt off. He put a hand out on to the floor to steady his alert crouch, which wasn't holding up very well. The sign changed itself again. It said:

DO NOT BE ALARMED.

After a pause, it added:

BE VERY, VERY FRIGHTENED, ARTHUR DENT.

Once again it flicked off. Once again it left him in darkness. His eyes seemed to be popping out of his head. He wasn't certain if this was because they were trying to see more clearly, or if they simply wanted to leave at this point.

'Hello?' he said again, this time trying to put a note of rugged and aggressive self-assertion into it. 'Is anyone there?'

There was no reply, nothing.

This unnerved Arthur even more than a reply would have done, and he began to back away from the scary nothingness. And the more he backed away, the more scared he became. After a while he realized that the reason for this was because of all the films he had seen in which the hero backs further and further away from some imagined terror in front of him, only to bump into it coming up from behind.

Just then it suddenly occurred to him to turn round rather quickly.

There was nothing there.

Just blackness.

This really unnerved him, and he started to back away from that, back the way he had come.

After doing this for a short while it suddenly occurred to him that he was now backing towards whatever it was he had been backing away from in the first place.

This, he couldn't help thinking, must be a foolish

thing to do. He decided he would be better off backing the way he had first been backing, and turned around again.

It turned out at this point that his second impulse had been the correct one, because there was an indescribably hideous monster dancing quietly behind him. Arthur yawed wildly as his skin tried to jump one way and his skeleton the other, whilst his brain tried to work out which of his ears it most wanted to crawl out of.

'Bet you weren't expecting to see me again,' said the monster, which Arthur couldn't help thinking was a strange remark for it to make, seeing as he had never met the creature before. He could tell that he hadn't met the creature before from the simple fact that he was able to sleep at nights. It was . . . it was . . . it was . . .

Arthur blinked at it. It stood very still. It did look a little familiar.

A terrible cold calm came over him as he realized that what he was looking at was a six-foot-high hologram of a housefly.

He wondered why anybody would be showing him a six-foot-high hologram of a housefly at this time. He wondered whose voice he had heard.

It was a terribly realistic hologram.

It vanished.

'Or perhaps you remember me better,' said the voice suddenly, and it was a deep, hollow malevolent voice which sounded like molten tar glurping out of a drum with evil on its mind, 'as the rabbit.'

With a sudden ping, there was a rabbit there in the black labyrinth with him, a huge, monstrously, hideously soft and lovable rabbit – an image again, but one on which every single soft and lovable hair seemed like a real and single thing growing in its soft and lovable coat. Arthur was startled to see his own reflection in its soft and lovable unblinking and extremely huge brown eye.

'Born in darkness,' rumbled the voice, 'raised in darkness. One morning I poked my head for the first time into the bright new world and got it split open by what felt suspiciously like some primitive instrument made of flint.

'Made by you, Arthur Dent, and wielded by you. Rather hard, as I recall.

'You turned my skin into a bag for keeping interesting stones in. I happen to know that because in my next life I came back as a fly again and you swatted me. Again. Only this time you swatted me with the bag you'd made of my previous skin.

'Arthur Dent, you are not merely a cruel and heartless man, you are also staggeringly tactless.'

The voice paused whilst Arthur gawped.

'I see you have lost the bag,' said the voice. 'Probably got bored with it, did you?'

Arthur shook his head helplessly. He wanted to explain that he had been in fact very fond of the bag and had looked after it very well and had taken it with him wherever he went, but that somehow every time he travelled anywhere he seemed inexplicably to end up with the wrong bag and that, curiously enough, even as they stood there he was just noticing for the first time that the bag he had with him at the moment appeared to be made out of rather nasty fake leopard skin, and wasn't the one he'd had a few moments ago before he arrived in this whatever place it was, and wasn't one he would have chosen himself and Heaven knew what would be in it as it wasn't his, and he would much rather have his original bag back, except that he was of course terribly sorry for having so peremptorily removed it, or rather its component parts, i.e. the rabbit skin, from its previous owner, viz. the rabbit whom he currently had the honour of attempting vainly to address.

All he actually managed to say was 'Erp.'

'Meet the newt you trod on,' said the voice.

And there was, standing in the corridor with Arthur, a giant green scaly newt. Arthur turned, yelped, leapt backwards, and found himself standing in the middle of the rabbit. He yelped again, but could find nowhere to leap to.

'That was me, too,' continued the voice in a low menacing rumble, 'as if you didn't know.'

'Know?' said Arthur with a start. 'Know?'

'The interesting thing about reincarnation,' rasped the voice, 'is that most people, most spirits, are not aware that it is happening to them.'

He paused for effect. As far as Arthur was concerned there was already quite enough effect going on.

'*I* was aware,' hissed the voice, 'that is, I *became* aware. Slowly. Gradually.'

He, whoever he was, paused again and gathered breath.

'I could hardly help it, could I,' he bellowed, 'when the same thing kept happening, over and over and over again! Every life I ever lived, I got killed by Arthur Dent. Any world, any body, any time, I'm just getting settled down, along comes Arthur Dent – pow, he kills me.

'Hard not to notice. Bit of a memory jogger. Bit of a pointer. Bit of a bloody giveaway!

'"That's funny," my spirit would say to itself as it winged its way back to the netherworld after another fruitless Dent-ended venture into the land of the living, "that man who just ran over me as I was hopping across the road to my favourite pond looked a little familiar . . ." And gradually I got to piece it together, Dent, you multiple-me-murderer!'

The echoes of his voice roared up and down the corridors. Arthur stood silent and cold, his head shaking with disbelief.

'Here's the moment, Dent,' shrieked the voice, now reaching a feverish pitch of hatred, 'here's the moment when at last I knew!'

It was indescribably hideous, the thing that suddenly opened up in front of Arthur, making him gasp and gargle with horror, but here's an attempt at a description of how hideous it was. It was a huge palpitating wet cave with a vast, slimy, rough, whale-like creature rolling around it and sliding over monstrous white tombstones. High above the cave rose a vast promontory in which could be seen the dark recesses of two further fearful caves, which . . .

Arthur Dent suddenly realized that he was looking at his own mouth, when his attention was meant to be directed at the live oyster that was being tipped helplessly into it.

He staggered back with a cry and averted his eyes.

When he looked again the appalling apparition had gone. The corridor was dark and, briefly, silent. He was alone with his thoughts. They were extremely unpleasant thoughts and would rather have had a chaperone.

The next noise, when it came, was the low heavy roll of a large section of wall trundling aside, revealing, for the moment, just dark blankness behind it. Arthur looked into it in much the same way that a mouse looks into a dark dog-kennel.

And the voice spoke to him again.

'Tell me it was a coincidence, Dent,' it said. 'I dare you to tell me it was a coincidence!'

'It *was* a coincidence,' said Arthur quickly.

'It was not!' came the answering bellow.

'It was,' said Arthur, 'it was . . .'

'If it was a coincidence, then my name,' roared the voice, 'is not Agrajag!!!'

'And presumably,' said Arthur, 'you would claim that that was your name.'

'Yes!' hissed Agrajag, as if he had just completed a rather deft syllogism.

'Well, I'm afraid it was still a coincidence,' said Arthur.

'Come in here and say that!' howled the voice, in sudden apoplexy again.

Arthur walked in and said that it was a coincidence, or at least, he nearly said that it was a coincidence. His tongue rather lost its footing towards the end of the last word because the lights came up and revealed what it was he had walked into.

It was a Cathedral of Hate.

It was the product of a mind that was not merely twisted, but actually sprained.

It was huge. It was horrific.

It had a Statue in it.

We will come to the Statue in a moment.

The vast, incomprehensibly vast, chamber looked as if it had been carved out of the inside of a mountain, and the reason for this was that that was precisely what it had been carved out of. It seemed to Arthur to spin sickeningly round his head as he stood and gaped at it.

It was black.

Where it wasn't black you were inclined to wish that it was, because the colours with which some of the unspeakable details were picked out ranged horribly across the whole spectrum of eye-defying colours, from Ultra Violent to Infra Dead.

The unspeakable details which these colours picked out were gargoyles which would have put Francis Bacon off his lunch.

The gargoyles all looked inwards from the walls, from the pillars, from the flying buttresses, from the choir stalls, towards the Statue, to which we will come in a moment.

And if the gargoyles would have put Francis Bacon off his lunch then it was clear from the gargoyles' faces that the Statue would have put them off theirs, had they been alive to eat it; which they weren't, and had anybody tried to serve them some, which they wouldn't.

Around the monumental walls were vast engraved stone tablets in memory of those who had fallen to Arthur Dent.

The names of some of those commemorated were underlined and had asterisks against them. So, for instance, the name of a cow which had been slaughtered and of which Arthur had happened to eat a fillet steak would have the plainest engraving, whereas the name of a fish which Arthur had himself caught and then decided he didn't like and left on the side of the plate had a double underlining, three sets of asterisks and a bleeding dagger added as decoration, just to make the point.

And what was most disturbing about all this, apart from the Statue, to which we are, by degrees, coming, was the very clear implication that all these people and creatures were indeed the same person, over and over again.

And it was equally clear that this person was, however unfairly, extremely upset and annoyed.

In fact it would be fair to say that he had reached a level of annoyance the like of which had never been seen in the Universe. It was an annoyance of epic proportions, a burning, searing flame of annoyance, an annoyance which now spanned the whole of time and space in its infinite umbrage.

And this annoyance had been given its fullest expression in the Statue in the centre of all this monstrosity, which was a statue of Arthur Dent, and an unflattering one. Fifty feet tall if it was an inch, there was not an inch of it which wasn't crammed with insult to its subject matter, and fifty feet of that sort of thing would be enough to make any subject feel bad. From the small pimple on the side of his nose to the poorish cut of his dressing gown, there was no aspect of Arthur Dent which wasn't lambasted and vilified by the sculptor.

Arthur appeared as a gorgon, an evil, rapacious, ravening, bloodied ogre, slaughtering his way through an innocent one-man Universe.

With each of the thirty arms which the sculptor in a fit of artistic fervour had decided to give him, he was either braining a rabbit, swatting a fly, pulling a wishbone, picking a flea out of his hair, or doing something which Arthur at first looking couldn't quite identify.

His many feet were mostly stamping on ants.

Arthur put his hands over his eyes, hung his head and shook it slowly from side to side in sadness and horror at the craziness of things.

And when he opened his eyes again, there in front of him stood the figure of the man or creature, or whatever it was, that he had supposedly been persecuting all this time.

'HhhhhhhrrrrrraaaaaaHHHHHH!' said Agrajag.

He, or it, or whatever, looked like a mad fat bat. He waddled slowly around Arthur, and poked at him with bent claws.

'Look . . .' protested Arthur.

'HhhhhhrrrrrraaaaaaHHHHHH!' explained Agrajag, and Arthur reluctantly accepted this on the grounds that he was rather frightened by this hideous and strangely wrecked apparition.

Agrajag was black, bloated, wrinkled and leathery.

His batwings were somehow more frightening for being the pathetic broken floundering things they were than if they had been strong, muscular beaters of the air. The frightening thing was probably the tenacity of his continued existence against all the physical odds.

He had the most astounding collection of teeth.

They looked as if they each came from a completely different animal, and they were ranged around his mouth at such bizarre angles it seemed that if he ever actually tried to chew anything he'd lacerate half his own face along with it, and possibly put an eye out as well.

Each of his three eyes was small and intense and looked about as sane as a fish in a privet bush.

'I was at a cricket match,' he rasped.

This seemed on the face of it such a preposterous notion that Arthur practically choked.

'Not in this body,' screeched the creature, 'not in this body! This is my last body. My last life. This is my revenge body. My kill-Arthur-Dent body. My last chance. I had to fight to get it, too.'

'But . . .'

'I was at,' roared Agrajag, 'a cricket match! I had a weak heart condition, but what, I said to my wife, can happen to me at a cricket match? As I'm watching, what happens?

'Two people quite maliciously appear out of thin air just in front of me. The last thing I can't help but notice before my poor heart gives out in shock is that one of them is Arthur Dent wearing a rabbit bone in his beard. Coincidence?'

'Yes,' said Arthur.

'Coincidence?' screamed the creature, painfully thrashing its broken wings, and opening a short gash on its right cheek with a particularly nasty tooth. On closer examination, such as he'd been hoping to avoid, Arthur noticed that much of Agrajag's face was covered with ragged strips of black sticky plasters.

He backed away nervously. He tugged at his beard. He was appalled to discover that in fact he still had the rabbit bone in it. He pulled it out and threw it away.

'Look,' he said, 'it's just fate playing silly buggers with you. With me. With me. It's a complete coincidence.'

'What have you got against me, Dent?' snarled the creature, advancing on him in a painful waddle.

'Nothing,' insisted Arthur, 'honestly, nothing.'

Agrajag fixed him with a beady stare.

'Seems a strange way to relate to somebody you've got nothing against, killing them all the time. Very curious piece of social interaction, I would call that. I'd also call it a lie!'

'But look,' said Arthur, 'I'm very sorry. There's been a terrible misunderstanding. I've got to go. Have you got a clock? I'm meant to be helping save the Universe.' He backed away still further.

Agrajag advanced still further.

'At one point,' he hissed, 'at one point, I decided to

give up. Yes. I would not come back. I would stay in the netherworld. And what happened?'

Arthur indicated with random shakes of his head that he had no idea and didn't want to have one either. He found he had backed up against the cold dark stone that had been carved by who knew what Herculean effort into a monstrous travesty of his bedroom slippers. He glanced up at his own horrendously parodied image towering above him. He was still puzzled as to what one of his hands was meant to be doing.

'I got yanked involuntarily back into the physical world,' pursued Agrajag, 'as a bunch of petunias. In, I might add, a bowl. This particular happy little lifetime started off with me, in my bowl, unsupported, three hundred miles above the surface of a particularly grim planet. Not a naturally tenable position for a bowl of petunias, you might think. And you'd be right. That life ended a very short while later, three hundred miles lower. In, I might again add, the fresh wreckage of a whale. My spirit brother.'

He leered at Arthur with renewed hatred.

'On the way down,' he snarled, 'I couldn't help noticing a flashy-looking white spaceship. And looking out of a port on this flashy-looking spaceship was a smug-looking Arthur Dent. *Coincidence?!!*'

'Yes!' yelped Arthur. He glanced up again, and realized that the arm that had puzzled him was represented as wantonly calling into existence a bowl of doomed petunias This was not a concept which leapt easily to the eye.

'I must go,' insisted Arthur.

'You may go,' said Agrajag, '*after* I have killed you.'

'No, that won't be any use,' explained Arthur, beginning to climb up the hard stone incline of his carved slipper, 'because I have to save the Universe, you see. I have to find a Silver Bail, that's the point. Tricky thing to do dead.'

'Save the Universe!' spat Agrajag with contempt. 'You should have thought of that before you started your vendetta against me! What about the time you were on Stavromula Beta and someone . . .'

'I've never been there,' said Arthur.

'. . . tried to assassinate you and you ducked. Who do you think the bullet bit? What did you say?'

'Never been there,' repeated Arthur. 'What are you talking about? I have to go.'

Agrajag stopped in his tracks.

'You must have been there. You were responsible for my death there, as everywhere else. An innocent bystander!' He quivered.

'I've never heard of the place,' insisted Arthur. 'I've certainly never had anyone try to assassinate me. Other than you. Perhaps I go there later, do you think?'

Agrajag blinked slowly in a kind of frozen logical horror.

'You haven't been to Stavromula Beta . . . *yet*?' he whispered.

'No,' said Arthur, 'I don't know anything about the place. Certainly never been to it, and don't have any plans to go.'

'Oh, you go there all right,' muttered Agrajag in a broken voice, 'you go there all right. Oh, Zark!' He tottered, and stared wildly about him at his huge Cathedral of Hate. 'I've brought you here too soon!'

He started to scream and bellow. 'I've brought you here too zarking soon!'

Suddenly he rallied, and turned a baleful, hating eye on Arthur.

'I'm going to kill you anyway!' he roared. 'Even if it's a logical impossibility I'm going to Zarking well try! I'm going to blow this whole mountain up!' He screamed, 'Let's see you get out of this one, Dent!'

He rushed in a painful waddling hobble to what appeared to be a small black sacrificial altar. He was shouting so wildly now that he was really carving his face up badly. Arthur leaped down from his vantage place on the carving of his own foot and ran to try to restrain the three-quarters-crazed creature.

He leaped upon him, and brought the strange monstrosity crashing down on top of the altar.

Agrajag screamed again, thrashed wildly for a brief moment, and turned a wild eye on Arthur.

'You know what you've done? he gurgled painfully. 'You've only gone and killed me again. I mean, what do you want from me, blood?'

He thrashed again in a brief apoplectic fit, quivered, and collapsed, smacking a large red button on the altar as he did so.

Arthur started with horror and fear, first at what he appeared to have done, and then at the loud sirens and bells that suddenly shattered the air to announce some clamouring emergency. He stared wildly around him.

The only exit appeared to be the way he came in. He pelted towards it, throwing away the nasty fake leopard skin bag as he did so.

He dashed randomly, haphazardly through the labyrinthine maze, he seemed to be pursued more and more fiercely by claxons, sirens, flashing lights.

Suddenly, he turned a corner and there was a light in front of him.

It wasn't flashing. It was daylight.

19

Although it has been said that on Earth alone in our Galaxy is Krikkit (or cricket) treated as fit subject for a game, and that for this reason the Earth has been shunned, this does only apply to our Galaxy, and more specifically to our dimension. In some of the higher dimensions they feel they can more or less please themselves, and have been playing a peculiar game called Brockian Ultra-Cricket for whatever their transdimensional equivalent of billions of years is.

'Let's be blunt, it's a nasty game' (says *The Hitchhiker's Guide to the Galaxy*), 'but then anyone who has been to any of the higher dimensions will know that they're a pretty nasty heathen lot up there who should just be smashed and done in, and would be, too, if anyone could work out a way of firing missiles at right angles to reality.'

This is another example of the fact that *The Hitchhiker's Guide to the Galaxy* will employ anybody who wants to walk straight in off the street and get ripped off, especially if they happen to walk in off the street during the afternoon, very few of the regular staff are there.

There is a fundamental point here:

The history of *The Hitchhiker's Guide to the Galaxy* is one of idealism, struggle, despair, passion, success, failure and enormously long lunch-breaks.

The earliest origins of the *Guide* are now, along with most of its financial records, lost in the mists of time.

For other, and more curious theories about where they are lost, see below.

Most of the surviving stories, however, speak of a founding editor called Hurling Frootmig.

Hurling Frootmig, it is said, founded the *Guide*, established its fundamental principles of honesty and idealism, and went bust.

There followed many years of penury and heart-searching during which he consulted friends, sat in darkened rooms in illegal states of mind, thought about this and that, fooled about with weights, and then, after a chance encounter with the Holy Lunching Friars of Voondoon (who claimed that just as lunch was at the centre of a man's temporal day, and man's temporal day could be seen as an analogy for his spiritual life, so lunch should

(a) be seen as the centre of a man's spiritual life, and

(b) be held in jolly nice restaurants), he refounded the *Guide*, laid down its fundamental principles of honesty and idealism and where you could stuff them both, and led the *Guide* on to its first major commercial success.

He also started to develop and explore the role of the editorial lunch-break which was subsequently to play such a crucial part in the *Guide*'s history, since it meant that most of the actual work got done by any passing stranger who happened to wander into the empty offices of an afternoon and saw something worth doing.

Shortly after this, the *Guide* was taken over by Megadodo Publications of Ursa Minor Beta, thus putting the whole thing on a very sound financial footing, and allowing the fourth editor, Lig Lury Jr, to embark on lunch-breaks of such breathtaking scope that even the efforts of recent editors, who have started undertaking sponsored lunch-breaks for charity, seem like mere sandwiches in comparison.

In fact, Lig never formally resigned his editorship – he merely left his office late one morning and has never since returned. Though well over a century has now passed, many members of the *Guide* staff still retain the romantic notion that he has simply popped out for a ham croissant, and will yet return to put in a solid afternoon's work.

Strictly speaking, all editors since Lig Lury Jr have therefore been designated Acting Editors, and Lig's desk is still preserved the way he left it, with the addition of a small sign which says 'Lig Lury Jr, Editor, Missing, presumed Fed'.

Some very scurrilous and subversive sources hint at the idea that Lig actually perished in the *Guide*'s first extraordinary experiments in alternative book-keeping. Very little is known of this, and less still said. Anyone who even notices, let alone calls attention to, the curious but utterly coincidental and meaningless fact that every world on which the *Guide* has ever set up an accounting department has shortly afterwards perished in warfare or some natural disaster is liable to get sued to smithereens.

It is an interesting though utterly unrelated fact that the two or three days prior to the demolition of the planet Earth to make way for a new hyperspace bypass saw a dramatic upsurge in the number of UFO sightings there, not only above Lord's Cricket Ground in St John's Wood, London, but also above Glastonbury in Somerset.

Glastonbury had long been associated with myths of ancient kings, witchcraft, ley-lines and wart curing, and had now been selected as the site for the new *Hitchhiker's Guide* financial records office, and indeed, ten years' worth of financial records were transferred to a magic hill just outside the city mere hours before the Vogons arrived.

None of these facts, however strange or inexplicable,

is as strange or inexplicable as the rules of the game of Brockian Ultra-Cricket, as played in the higher dimensions. A full set of rules is so massively complicated that the only time they were all bound together in a single volume, they underwent gravitational collapse and became a black hole.

A brief summary, however, is as follows:

RULE ONE: Grow at least three extra legs. You won't need them, but it keeps the crowds amused.

RULE TWO: Find one good Brockian Ultra-Cricket player. Clone him off a few times. This saves an enormous amount of tedious selection and training.

RULE THREE: Put your team and the opposing team in a large field and build a high wall round them.

The reason for this is that, though the game is a major spectator sport, the frustration experienced by the audience at not actually being able to see what's going on leads them to imagine that it's a lot more exciting than it really is. A crowd that has just watched a rather humdrum game experiences far less life-affirmation than a crowd that believes it has just missed the most dramatic event in sporting history.

RULE FOUR: Throw lots of assorted items of sporting equipment over the wall for the players. Anything will do – cricket bats, basecube bats, tennis guns, skis, anything you can get a good swing with.

RULE FIVE: The players should now lay about themselves for all they are worth with whatever they find to hand. Whenever a player scores a 'hit' on another player, he should immediately run away and apologize from a safe distance.

Apologies should be concise, sincere and, for maximum clarity and points, delivered through a megaphone.

RULE SIX: The winning team shall be the first team that wins.

Curiously enough, the more the obsession with the game grows in the higher dimensions, the less it is actually played, since most of the competing teams are now in a state of permanent warfare with each other over the interpretation of these rules. This is all for the best, because in the long run a good solid war is less psychologically damaging than a protracted game of Brockian Ultra-Cricket.

20

As Arthur ran darting, and panting down the side of the mountain he suddenly felt the whole bulk of the mountain move very very slightly beneath him. There was a rumble, a roar, and a slight blurred movement; and a lick of heat in the distance behind and above him. He ran in a frenzy of fear. The land began to slide, and he suddenly felt the force of the word 'landslide' in a way which had never been apparent to him before. It had always just been a word to him, but now he was suddenly and horribly aware that sliding is a strange and sickening thing for land to do. It was doing it with him on it. He felt ill with fear and shaking. The ground slid, the mountain slurred, he slipped, he fell, he stood, he slipped again and ran. The avalanche began.

Stones, then rocks, then boulders which pranced past him like clumsy puppies, only much, much bigger, much, much harder and heavier, and almost infinitely more likely to kill you if they fell on you. His eyes danced with them, his feet danced with the dancing ground. He ran as if running was a terrible sweating sickness, his heart pounded to the rhythm of the pounding geological frenzy around him.

The logic of the situation, i.e. that he was clearly bound to survive if the next foreshadowed incident in the saga of his inadvertent persecution of Agrajag was to happen, was utterly failing to impinge itself on his mind or exercise any restraining influence on him at this time. He ran with the fear of death in him, under him, over him and grabbing hold of his hair.

And suddenly he tripped again and was hurled forward by his considerable momentum. But just at the moment that he was about to hit the ground astoundingly hard he saw lying directly in front of him a small navy-blue holdall that he knew for a fact he had lost in the baggage-retrieval system at Athens airport some ten years in his personal time-scale previously, and in his astonishment he missed the ground completely and bobbed off into the air with his brain singing.

What he was doing was this: he was flying. He glanced around him in surprise, but there could be no doubt that that was what he was doing. No part of him was touching the ground, and no part of him was even approaching it. He was simply floating there with boulders hurtling through the air around him.

He could now do something about that. Blinking with the non-effort of it he wafted higher into the air, and now the boulders were hurtling through the air beneath him.

He looked downwards with intense curiosity. Between him and the shivering ground were now some thirty feet of empty air, empty that is if you discounted the boulders which didn't stay in it for long, but bounded downwards in the iron grip of the law of gravity: the same law which seemed, all of a sudden, to have given Arthur a sabbatical.

It occurred to him almost instantly, with the instinctive correctness that self-preservation instils in the mind, that he mustn't try to think about it, that if he did, the law of gravity would suddenly glance sharply in his direction and demand to know what the hell he thought he was doing up there, and all would suddenly be lost.

So he thought about tulips. It was difficult, but he did. He thought about the pleasing firm roundness of the bottom of tulips, he thought about the interesting variety of colours they came in, and wondered what proportion of the total number of tulips that grew, or had grown, on the Earth would be found within a radius of one mile from a windmill. After a while he got dangerously bored with this train of thought, felt the air slipping away beneath him, felt that he was drifting down into the paths of the bouncing boulders that he was trying so hard not to think about, so he thought about Athens airport for a bit and that kept him usefully annoyed for about five minutes – at the end of which he was startled to discover that he was now floating about two hundred yards above the ground.

He wondered for a moment how he was going to get back down to it, but instantly shied away from that area of speculation again, and tried to look at the situation steadily.

He was flying. What was he going to do about it? He looked back down at the ground. He didn't look at it hard, but did his best just to give it an idle glance, as it were, in passing. There were a couple of things he couldn't help noticing. One was that the eruption of the mountain seemed now to have spent itself – there was a crater just a little way beneath the peak, presumably where the rock had caved in on top of the huge cavernous cathedral, the statue of himself, and the sadly abused figure of Agrajag.

The other was his hold-all, the one he had lost at Athens airport. It was sitting pertly on a piece of clear ground, surrounded by exhausted boulders but apparently hit by none of them. Why this should be he could not speculate, but since this mystery was completely overshadowed by the monstrous impossibility of the bag being there in the first place, it was not a speculation he really felt strong enough for anyway. The thing is, it was there. And the nasty, fake leopard-skin bag seemed to have disappeared, which was all to the good, if not entirely to the explicable.

He was faced with the fact that he was going to have to pick the thing up. Here he was, flying along two hundred yards above the surface of an alien planet the name of which he couldn't even remember. He could not ignore the plaintive posture of this tiny piece of what used to be his life, here, so many light-years from the pulverized remains of his home.

Furthermore, he realized, the bag, if it was still in the state in which he lost it, would contain a can which would have in it the only Greek olive oil still surviving in the Universe.

Slowly, carefully, inch by inch, he began to bob downwards, swinging gently from side to side like a nervous sheet of paper feeling its way towards the ground.

It went well, he was feeling good. The air supported him, but let him through. Two minutes later he was hovering a mere two feet above the bag, and was faced with some difficult decisions. He bobbed there lightly. He frowned, but again, as lightly as he could.

If he picked the bag up, could he carry it? Mightn't the extra weight just pull him straight to the ground?

Mightn't the mere act of touching something on the ground suddenly discharge whatever mysterious force it was that was holding him in the air?

Mightn't he be better off just being sensible at this point and stepping out of the air, back on to the ground for a moment or two?

If he did, would he ever be able to fly again?

The sensation, when he allowed himself to be aware of it, was so quietly ecstatic that he could not bear the thought of losing it, perhaps for ever. With this worry in mind he bobbed upwards a little again, just to try the feel of it, the surprising and effortless movement of it. He bobbed, he floated. He tried a little swoop.

The swoop was terrific. With his arms spread out in front of him, his hair and dressing gown streaming out behind him, he dived down out of the sky, bellied along a body of air about two feet from the ground and swung back up again, catching himself at the top of the swing and holding. Just holding. He stayed there.

It was wonderful.

And that, he realized, was the way of picking up the bag. He would swoop down and catch hold of it just at the point of the upswing. He would carry it on up with him. He might wobble a bit, but he was certain that he could hold it.

He tried one or two more practice swoops, and they got better and better. The air on his face, the bounce and woof of his body, all combined to make him feel an intoxication of the spirit that he hadn't felt since, since – well, as far as he could work out, since he was born. He drifted away on the breeze and surveyed the countryside, which was, he discovered, pretty nasty. It had a wasted ravaged look. He decided not to look at it any more. He would just pick up the bag and then ... he didn't know what he was going to do after he had picked up the bag. He decided he would just pick up the bag and see where things went from there.

He judged himself against the wind, pushed up against it and turned around. He floated on its body. He didn't realize, but his body was willoming at this point.

He ducked down under the airstream, dipped – and dived.

The air threw itself past him, he thrilled through it. The ground wobbled uncertainly, straightened its ideas out and rose smoothly up to meet him, offering the bag, its cracked plastic handles up towards him.

Halfway down there was a sudden dangerous moment when he could no longer believe he was doing this, and therefore he very nearly wasn't, but he recovered himself in time, skimmed over the ground, slipped an arm smoothly through the handles of the bag, and began to climb back up, couldn't make it and all of a sudden collapsed, bruised, scratched and shaking on the stony ground.

He staggered instantly to his feet and swayed hopelessly around, swinging the bag around him in an agony of grief and disappointment.

His feet, suddenly, were stuck heavily to the ground in the way they always had been. His body seemed like an unwieldy sack of potatoes that reeled stumbling against the ground, his mind had all the lightness of a bag of lead.

He sagged and swayed and ached with giddiness. He tried hopelessly to run, but his legs were suddenly too weak. He tripped and flopped forward. At that moment he remembered that in the bag he was now carrying was not only a can of Greek olive oil but a duty-free allowance of retsina, and in the pleasurable shock of that realization he failed to notice for at best ten seconds that he was now flying again.

He whooped and cried with relief and pleasure, and sheer physical delight. He swooped, he wheeled, he skidded and whirled through the air. Cheekily he sat on an updraught and went through the contents of the hold-all. He felt the way he imagined an angel must feel doing its celebrated dance on the head of a pin whilst being counted by philosophers. He laughed with pleasure at the discovery that the bag did in fact contain the olive oil and the retsina as well as a pair of cracked sunglasses, some sand-filled swimming trunks, some creased postcards of Santorini, a large and unsightly towel, some interesting stones, and various scraps of paper with the addresses of people he was relieved to think he would never meet again, even if the reason why was a sad one. He dropped the stones, put on the sunglasses, and let the pieces of paper whip away in the wind.

Ten minutes later, drifting idly through a cloud, he got a large and extremely disreputable cocktail party in the small of the back.

21

The longest and most destructive party ever held is now into its fourth generation and still no one shows any signs of leaving. Somebody did once look at his watch, but that was eleven years ago now, and there has been no follow-up.

The mess is extraordinary, and has to be seen to be

believed, but if you don't have any particular need to believe it, then don't go and look, because you won't enjoy it.

There have recently been some bangs and flashes up in the clouds, and there is one theory that this is a battle being fought between the fleets of several rival carpet-cleaning companies who are hovering over the thing like vultures, but you shouldn't believe anything you hear at parties, and particularly not anything you hear at this one.

One of the problems, and it's one which is obviously going to get worse, is that all the people at the party are either the children or the grandchildren or the great-grandchildren of the people who wouldn't leave in the first place, and because of all the business about selective breeding and regressive genes and so on, it means that all the people now at the party are either absolutely fanatical partygoers, or gibbering idiots, or, more and more frequently, both.

Either way, it means that, genetically speaking, each succeeding generation is now less likely to leave than the preceding one.

So other factors come into operation, like when the drink is going to run out.

Now, because of certain things which have happened which seemed like a good idea at the time (and one of the problems with a party which never stops is that all the things which only seem like a good idea at parties continue to seem like good ideas), that point seems still to be a long way off.

One of the things which seemed like a good idea at the time was that the party should fly – not in the normal sense that parties are meant to fly, but literally.

One night, long ago, a band of drunken astro-engineers of the first generation clambered round the building digging this, fixing that, banging very hard on the other, and when the sun rose the following morning, it was startled to find itself shining on a building full of happy drunken people which was now floating like a young and uncertain bird over the treetops.

Not only that, but the flying party had also managed to arm itself rather heavily. If they were going to get involved in any petty arguments with wine merchants, they wanted to make sure they had might on their side.

The transition from full-time cocktail party to part-time raiding party came with ease, and did much to add that extra bit of zest and swing to the whole affair which was badly needed at this point because of the enormous number of times that the band had already played all the numbers it knew over the years.

They looted, they raided, they held whole cities to ransom for fresh supplies of cheese crackers, avocado dip, spare ribs and wine and spirits, which would now get piped aboard from floating tankers.

The problem of when the drink is going to run out is, however, going to have to be faced one day.

The planet over which they are floating is no longer the planet it was when they first started floating over it.

It is in bad shape.

The party has attacked and raided an awful lot of it, and no one has ever succeeded in hitting it back because of the erratic and unpredictable way in which it lurches round the sky.

It is one hell of a party.

It is also one hell of a thing to get hit by in the small of the back.

22

Arthur lay floundering in pain on a piece of ripped and dismembered reinforced concrete, flicked at by wisps of passing cloud and confused by the sounds of flabby merrymaking somewhere indistinctly behind him.

There was a sound he couldn't immediately identify, partly because he didn't know the tune 'I Left my Leg in Jaglan Beta' and partly because the band playing it were very tired, and some members of it were playing in three-four time, some in four-four, and some in a kind of pie-eyed πr^2, each according to the amount of sleep he'd managed to grab recently.

He lay, panting heavily in the wet air, and tried feeling bits of himself to see where he might be hurt. Wherever he touched himself, he encountered a pain. After a short while he worked out that this was because it was his hand that was hurting. He seemed to have sprained his wrist. His back, too, was hurting, but he soon satisfied himself that he was not badly hurt, but just bruised and a little shaken, as who wouldn't be? He couldn't understand what a building would be doing flying through the clouds.

On the other hand, he would have been a little hard-pressed to come up with any convincing explanation of his own presence, so he decided that he and the building were just going to have to accept each other. He looked up from where he was lying. A wall of pale but stained stone slabs rose up behind him, the building proper. He seemed to be stretched out on some sort of ledge or lip which extended outwards for about three or four feet all the way around. It was a hunk of the ground in which the party building had had its foundations, and which it had taken along with itself to keep itself bound together at the bottom end.

Nervously, he stood up and, suddenly, looking out over the edge, he felt nauseous with vertigo. He pressed himself back against the wall, wet with mist and sweat. His head was swimming freestyle, but someone in his stomach was doing the butterfly.

Even though he had got up here under his own power, he could now not even bear to contemplate the hideous drop in front of him. He was not about to try his luck jumping. He was not about to move an inch closer to the edge.

Clutching his hold-all he edged along the wall, hoping to find a doorway in. The solid weight of the can of olive oil was a great reassurance to him.

He was edging in the direction of the nearest corner, in the hope that the wall around the corner might offer more in the way of entrances than this one, which offered none.

The unsteadiness of the building's flight made him feel sick with fear, and after a short time he took the towel from out of his holdall and did something with it which once again justified its supreme position in the list of useful things to take with you when you hitch hike round the Galaxy. He put it over his head so he wouldn't have to see what he was doing.

His feet edged along the ground. His outstretched hand edged along the wall.

Finally he came to the corner, and as his hand rounded the corner it encountered something which gave him such a shock that he nearly fell straight off. It was another hand.

The two hands gripped each other.

He desperately wanted to use his other hand to pull the towel back from his eyes, but it was holding the hold-all with the olive oil, the retsina and the postcards of Santorini, and he very much didn't want to put it down.

He experienced one of those 'self' moments, one of those moments when you suddenly turn around and look at yourself and think: 'Who am I? What am I up to? What have I achieved? Am I doing well?' He whimpered very slightly.

He tried to free his hand, but he couldn't. The other hand was holding his tightly. He had no recourse but to edge onwards towards the corner. He leaned around it and shook his head in an attempt to dislodge the towel. This seemed to provoke a sharp cry of some unfathomable emotion from the owner of the other hand.

The towel was whipped from his head and he found his eyes peering into those of Ford Prefect. Beyond him stood Slartibartfast, and beyond them he could clearly see a porchway and a large closed door.

They were both pressed back against the wall, eyes wild with terror as they stared out into the thick blind cloud around them, and tried to resist the lurching and swaying of the building.

'Where the Zarking photon have you been?' hissed Ford, panic stricken.

'Er, well,' stuttered Arthur, not really knowing how to sum it all up that briefly. 'Here and there. What are you doing here?'

Ford turned his wild eyes on Arthur again.

'They won't let us in without a bottle,' he hissed.

The first thing Arthur noticed as they entered into the thick of the party, apart from the noise, the suffocating heat, the wild profusion of colours that protruded dimly through the atmosphere of heady smoke, the carpets thick with ground glass, ash and avocado droppings, and the small group of pterodactyl-like creatures in lurex who descended on his cherished bottle of retsina, squawking, 'A new pleasure, a new pleasure', was Trillian being chatted up by a Thunder God.

'Didn't I see you at Milliways?' he was saying.

'Were you the one with the hammer?'

'Yes. I much prefer it here. So much less reputable, so much more fraught.'

Squeals of some hideous pleasure rang around the room, the outer dimensions of which were invisible through the heaving throng of happy, noisy creatures, cheerfully yelling things that nobody could hear at each other and occasionally having crises.

'Seems fun,' said Trillian 'What did you say, Arthur?'

'I said, how the hell did you get here?'

'I was a row of dots flowing randomly through the Universe. Have you met Thor? He makes thunder.'

'Hello,' said Arthur. 'I expect that must be very interesting.'

'Hi,' said Thor. 'It is. Have you got a drink?'

'Er, no actually . . .'

'Then why don't you go and get one?'

'See you later, Arthur,' said Trillian.

Something jogged Arthur's mind, and he looked around huntedly.

'Zaphod isn't here, is he?' he said.

'See you,' said Trillian firmly, 'later.'

Thor glared at him with hard coal-black eyes, his beard bristled, what little light there was in the place mustered its forces briefly to glint menacingly off the horns on his helmet.

He took Trillian's elbow in his extremely large hand

and the muscles in his upper arm moved around each other like a couple of Volkswagens parking.

He led her away.

'One of the interesting things about being immortal,' he said, 'is . . .'

'One of the interesting things about space,' Arthur heard Slartibartfast saying to a large and voluminous creature who looked like someone losing a fight with a pink duvet and was gazing raptly at the old man's deep eyes and silver beard, 'is how dull it is.'

'Dull?' said the creature, and blinked her rather wrinkled and bloodshot eyes.

'Yes,' said Slartibartfast, 'staggeringly dull. Bewilderingly so. You see, there's so much of it and so little in it. Would you like me to quote you some statistics?'

'Er, well . . .'

'Please, I would like to. They, too, are quite sensationally dull.'

'I'll come back and hear them in a moment,' she said, patted him on the arm, lifted up her skirts like a hovercraft and moved off into the heaving crowd.

'I thought she'd never go,' growled the old man. 'Come, Earthman . . .'

'Arthur.'

'We must find the Silver Bail, it is here somewhere.'

'Can't we just relax a little?' Arthur said. 'I've had a tough day. Trillian's here, incidentally, she didn't say how, it probably doesn't matter.'

'Think of the danger to the Universe . . .'

'The Universe,' said Arthur, 'is big enough and old enough to look after itself for half an hour. All right,' he added, in response to Slartibartfast's increasing agitation, 'I'll wander round and see if anybody's seen it.'

'Good, good,' said Slartibartfast, 'good.' He plunged

into the crowd himself, and was told to relax by everybody he passed.

'Have you seen a bail anywhere?' said Arthur to a little man who seemed to be standing eagerly waiting to listen to somebody. 'It's made of silver, vitally important for the future safety of the Universe, and about this long.'

'No,' said the enthusiastically wizened little man, 'but do have a drink and tell me all about it.'

Ford Prefect writhed past, dancing a wild, frenetic and not entirely unobscene dance with someone who looked as if she was wearing Sydney Opera House on her head. He was yelling a futile conversation at her above the din.

'I like the hat!' he bawled.

'What?'

'I said, I like the hat.'

'I'm not wearing a hat.'

'Well, I like the head then.'

'What?'

'I said, I like the head. Interesting bone structure.'

'What?'

Ford worked a shrug into the complex routine of other movements he was performing.

'I said, you dance great,' he shouted, 'just don't nod so much.'

'What?'

'It's just that every time you nod,' said Ford, '. . . ow!' he added as his partner nodded forward to say 'What? and once again pecked him sharply on the forehead with the sharp end of her swept-forward skull.

'My planet was blown up one morning,' said Arthur, who had found himself quite unexpectedly telling the little man his life story or, at least, edited highlights of it, 'that's why I'm dressed like this, in my dressing gown. My planet was blown up with all my clothes in it, you see. I didn't realize I'd be coming to a party.'

The little man nodded enthusiastically.

'Later, I was thrown off a spaceship. Still in my dressing gown, rather than the space suit one would normally expect. Shortly after that I discovered that my planet had originally been built for a bunch of mice. You can imagine how I felt about that. I was then shot at for a while and blown up. In fact I have been blown up ridiculously often, shot at, insulted, regularly disintegrated, deprived of tea, and recently I crashed into a swamp and had to spend five years in a damp cave.'

'Ah,' effervesced the little man, 'and did you have a wonderful time?'

Arthur started to choke violently on his drink.

'What a wonderfully exciting cough,' said the little man, quite startled by it, 'do you mind if I join you?'

And with that he launched into the most extraordinary and spectacular fit of coughing which caught Arthur so much by surprise that he started to choke violently, discovered he was already doing it and got thoroughly confused.

Together they performed a lung-busting duet which went on for fully two minutes before Arthur managed to cough and splutter to a halt.

'So invigorating,' said the little man, panting and wiping tears from his eyes. 'What an exciting life you must lead. Thank you very much.'

He shook Arthur warmly by the hand and walked off into the crowd. Arthur shook his head in astonishment.

A youngish-looking man came up to him, an aggressive-looking type with a hook mouth, a lantern nose, and small beady little cheekbones. He was wearing black trousers, a black silk shirt open to what was presumably his navel, though Arthur had learnt never to make assumptions about the anatomies of the sort of people he tended to meet these days, and had all sorts of nasty dangly gold things hanging round his neck. He carried something in a black bag, and clearly wanted people to notice that he didn't want them to notice it.

'Hey, er, did I hear you say your name just now?' he said.

This was one of the many things that Arthur had told the enthusiastic little man.

'Yes, it's Arthur Dent.'

The man seemed to be dancing slightly to some rhythm other than any of the several that the band were grimly pushing out.

'Yeah,' he said, 'only there was a man in a mountain wanted to see you.'

'I met him.'

'Yeah, only he seemed pretty anxious about it, you know.'

'Yes, I met him.'

'Yeah, well I think you should know that.'

'I do. I met him.'

The man paused to chew a little gum. Then he clapped Arthur on the back.

'OK,' he said, 'all right. I'm just telling you, right? Good night, good luck, win awards.'

'What?' said Arthur, who was beginning to flounder seriously at this point.

'Whatever. Do what you do. Do it well.' He made a sort of clucking noise with whatever he was chewing and then some vaguely dynamic gesture.

'Why?' said Arthur.

'Do it badly,' said the man, 'who cares? Who gives a shit?' The blood suddenly seemed to pump angrily into the man's face and he started to shout.

'Why not go mad?' he said. 'Go away, get off my back will you, guy. Just Zark off!!!'

'OK, I'm going,' said Arthur hurriedly.

'It's been real.' The man gave a sharp wave and disappeared off into the throng.

'What was that about?' said Arthur to a girl he found standing beside him. 'Why did he tell me to win awards?'

'Just showbiz talk,' shrugged the girl. 'He's just won an award at the Annual Ursa Minor Alpha Recreational Illusions Institute Awards Ceremony, and was hoping to be able to pass it off lightly, only you didn't mention it, so he couldn't.'

'Oh,' said Arthur, 'oh, well I'm sorry I didn't. What was it for?'

'The Most Gratuitous Use Of The Word "Fuck" In A Serious Screenplay. It's very prestigious.'

'I see,' said Arthur, 'yes, and what do you get for that?'

'A Rory. It's just a small silver thing set on a large black base. What did you say?'

'I didn't say anything, I was just about to ask what the silver . . .'

'Oh, I thought you said "wop".'

'Said what?'

'Wop.'

People had been dropping in on the party now for some years, fashionable gatecrashers from other worlds, and for some time it had occurred to the partygoers as they had looked out at their own world beneath them, with its wrecked cities, its ravaged avocado farms and blighted vineyards, its vast tracts of new desert, its seas full of biscuit crumbs and worse, that their world was in some tiny and almost imperceptible ways not quite as much fun as it had been. Some of them had begun to wonder if they could manage to stay sober for long enough to make the entire party spaceworthy and maybe take it off to some other people's worlds where the air might be fresher and give them fewer headaches.

The few undernourished farmers who still managed to scratch out a feeble existence on the half-dead ground of the planet's surface would have been extremely pleased to hear this, but that day, as the party came screaming out of the clouds and the farmers looked up in haggard fear of yet another cheese-and-wine raid, it became clear that the party was not going to be going anywhere else for a while, that the party would soon be over. Very soon it would be time to gather up hats and coats and stagger blearily outside to find out what time of day it was, what time of year it was, and whether in any of this burnt and ravaged land there was a taxi going anywhere.

The party was locked in a horrible embrace with a strange white spaceship which seemed to be half sticking through it. Together they were lurching, heaving and spinning their way round the sky in grotesque disregard of their own weight.

The clouds parted. The air roared and leapt out of their way.

The party and the Krikkit warship looked, in their writhings, a little like two ducks, one of which is trying to make a third duck inside the second duck, whilst the second duck is trying very hard to explain that it doesn't feel ready for a third duck right now, is uncertain that it would want any putative third duck to be made by this particular first duck anyway, and certainly not whilst it, the second duck, was busy flying.

The sky sang and screamed with the rage of it all and buffeted the ground with shock waves.

And suddenly, with a foop, the Krikkit ship was gone.

The party blundered helplessly across the sky like a man leaning against an unexpectedly open door. It span and wobbled on its hover jets. It tried to right itself and wronged itself instead. It staggered back across the sky again.

For a while these staggerings continued, but clearly they could not continue for long. The party was now a mortally wounded party. All the fun had gone out of it, as the occasional broken-backed pirouette could not disguise.

The longer, at this point, that it avoided the ground, the heavier was going to be the crash when finally it hit it.

Inside, things were not going well either. They were going monstrously badly, in fact, and people were hating it and saying so loudly. The Krikkit robots had been.

They had removed the Award for The Most Gratuitous Use Of The Word 'Fuck' In A Serious Screenplay, and in its place had left a scene of devastation that left Arthur feeling almost as sick as a runner-up for a Rory.

'We would love to stay and help,' shouted Ford, picking his way over the mangled debris, 'only we're not going to.'

The party lurched again, provoking feverish cries and groans from amongst the smoking wreckage.

'We have to go and save the Universe, you see,' said Ford. 'And if that sounds like a pretty lame excuse, then you may be right. Either way, we're off.'

He suddenly came across an unopened bottle lying, miraculously unbroken, on the ground.

'Do you mind if we take this?' he said. 'You won't be needing it.'

He took a packet of potato crisps too.

'Trillian?' shouted Arthur in a shocked and weakened voice. In the smoking mess he could see nothing.

'Earthmen, we must go,' said Slartibartfast nervously.

'Trillian?' shouted Arthur again.

A moment or two later, Trillian staggered, shaking, into view, supported by her new friend the Thunder God.

'The girl stays with me,' said Thor. 'There's a great party going on in Valhalla, we'll be flying off . . .'

'Where were you when all this was going on?' said Arthur.

'Upstairs,' said Thor, 'I was weighing her. Flying's a tricky business you see, you have to calculate wind . . .'

'She comes with us,' said Arthur.

'Hey,' said Trillian, 'don't I . . .'

'No,' said Arthur, 'you come with us.'

Thor looked at him with slowly smouldering eyes. He was making some point about godliness and it had nothing to do with being clean.

'She comes with me,' he said quietly.

'Come on, Earthman,' said Slartibartfast nervously, picking at Arthur's sleeve.

'Come on, Slartibartfast,' said Ford nervously, picking at the old man's sleeve. Slartibartfast had the teleport device.

The party lurched and swayed, sending everyone reeling, except for Thor and except for Arthur, who stared, shaking, into the Thunder God's black eyes.

Slowly, incredibly, Arthur put up what now appeared to be his tiny little fists.

'Want to make something of it?' he said.

'I beg your minuscule pardon?' roared Thor.

'I said,' repeated Arthur, and he could not keep the quavering out of his voice, 'do you want to make something of it?' He waggled his fists ridiculously.

Thor looked at him with incredulity. Then a little wisp of smoke curled upwards from his nostril. There was a tiny little flame in it too.

He gripped his belt.

He expanded his chest to make it totally clear that here was the sort of man you only dared to cross if you had a team of Sherpas with you.

He unhooked the shaft of his hammer from his belt. He held it up in his hands to reveal the massive iron head. He thus cleared up any possible misunderstanding that he might merely have been carrying a telegraph pole around with him.

'Do I want,' he said, with a hiss like a river flowing through a steel mill, 'to make something of it?'

'Yes,' said Arthur, his voice suddenly and extraordinarily strong and belligerent. He waggled his fists again, this time as if he meant it.

'You want to step outside? he snarled at Thor.

'All right!' bellowed Thor, like an enraged bull (or in fact like an enraged Thunder God, which is a great deal more impressive), and did so.

'Good,' said Arthur, 'that's got rid of him. Slarty, get us out of here.'

23

'All right,' shouted Ford at Arthur, 'so I'm a coward, the point is I'm still alive.' They were back aboard the *Starship Bistromath*. So was Slartibartfast. So was Trillian. Harmony and concord were not.

'Well, so am I alive, aren't I?' retaliated Arthur, haggard with adventure and anger. His eyebrows were leaping up and down as if they wanted to punch each other.

'You damn nearly weren't,' exploded Ford.

Arthur turned sharply to Slartibartfast, who was sitting in his pilot couch on the flight deck gazing thoughtfully into the bottom of a bottle which was telling him something he clearly couldn't fathom. He appealed to him.

'Do you think he understands the first word I've been saying?' he said, quivering with emotion.

'I don't know,' replied Slartibartfast, a little abstractedly. 'I'm not sure,' he added, glancing up very briefly, 'that I do.' He stared at his instruments with renewed vigour and bafflement. 'You'll have to explain it to us again,' he said.

'Well . . .'

'But later. Terrible things are afoot.'

He tapped the pseudo-glass of the bottle bottom.

'We fared rather pathetically at the party, I'm afraid,' he said, 'and our only hope now is to try to prevent the robots from using the Key in the Lock. How in heaven we do that I don't know,' he muttered. 'Just have to go there, I suppose. Can't say I like the idea at all. Probably end up dead.'

'Where is Trillian anyway?' said Arthur with a sudden affectation of unconcern. What he had been angry about was that Ford had berated him for wasting time over all the business with the Thunder God when they could have been making a rather more rapid escape. Arthur's own opinion, and he had offered it for whatever anybody might have felt it was worth, was that he had been extraordinarily brave and resourceful.

The prevailing view seemed to be that his opinion was not worth a pair of fetid dingo's kidneys. What really hurt, though, was that Trillian didn't seem to react much one way or the other and had wandered off somewhere.

'And where are my potato crisps?' said Ford.

'They are both,' said Slartibartfast without looking up, 'in the Room of Informational Illusions. I think that your young lady friend is trying to understand some problems of Galactic history. I think the potato crisps are probably helping her.'

24

It is a mistake to think you can solve any major problems just with potatoes.

For instance, there was once an insanely aggressive race of people called the Silastic Armorfiends of Striterax. That was just the name of their race. The name of their army was something quite horrific. Luckily they lived even further back in Galactic history than anything we have so far encountered – twenty billion years ago – when the Galaxy was young and fresh and every idea worth fighting for was a new one.

And fighting was what the Silastic Armorfiends of Striterax were good at, and being good at it, they did it a lot. They fought their enemies (i.e. everybody else), they fought each other. Their planet was a complete wreck. The surface was littered with abandoned cities which were surrounded by abandoned war machines, which were in turn surrounded by deep bunkers in which the Silastic Armorfiends lived and squabbled with each other.

The best way to pick a fight with a Silastic Armorfiend of Striterax was just to be born. They didn't like it, they got resentful. And when an Armorfiend got resentful, someone got hurt. An exhausting way of life, one might think, but they did seem to have an awful lot of energy.

The best way of dealing with a Silastic Armorfiend was to put him in a room on his own, because sooner or later he would simply beat himself up.

Eventually they realized that this was something they were going to have to sort out, and they passed a law decreeing that anyone who had to carry a weapon as part of his normal Silastic work (policemen, security guards, primary-school teachers, etc.) had to spend at least forty-five minutes every day punching a sack of potatoes in order to work off his or her surplus aggression.

For a while this worked well, until someone thought that it would be much more efficient and less time consuming if they just shot the potatoes instead.

This led to a renewed enthusiasm for shooting all sorts of things, and they all got very excited at the prospect of their first major war for weeks.

Another achievement of the Silastic Armorfiends of Striterax is that they were the first race who ever managed to shock a computer.

It was a gigantic spaceborne computer called Hactar, which to this day is remembered as one of the most powerful ever built. It was the first to be built like a natural brain, in that every cellular particle of it carried the pattern of the whole within it, which enabled it to think more flexibly and imaginatively, and also, it seemed, to be shocked.

The Silastic Armorfiends of Striterax were engaged in one of their regular wars with the Strenuous Garfighters of Stug, and were not enjoying it as much as usual because it involved an awful lot of trekking through the Radiation Swamps of Cwulzenda, and across the Fire

Mountains of FrazFraga, neither of which terrains they felt at home in.

So when the Strangulous Stilettans of Jajazikstak joined in the fray and forced them to fight another front in the Gamma Caves of Carfrax and the Ice Storms of Varlengooten, they decided that enough was enough, and they ordered Hactar to design for them an Ultimate Weapon.

'What do you mean,' asked Hactar, 'by Ultimate?'

To which the Silastic Armorfiends of Striterax said, 'Read a bloody dictionary,' and plunged back into the fray.

So Hactar designed an Ultimate Weapon.

It was a very, very small bomb which was simply a junction box in hyperspace that would, when activated, connect the heart of every major sun with the heart of every other major sun simultaneously and thus turn the entire Universe into one gigantic hyperspatial supernova.

When the Silastic Armorfiends tried to use it to blow up a Strangulous Stilettan munitions dump in one of the Gamma Caves, they were extremely irritated that it didn't work, and said so.

Hactar had been shocked by the whole idea.

He tried to explain that he had been thinking about this Ultimate Weapon business, and had worked out that there was no conceivable consequence of not setting the bomb off that was worse than the known consequence of setting it off, and he had therefore taken the liberty of introducing a small flaw into the design of the bomb, and he hoped that everyone involved would, on sober reflection, feel that . . .

The Silastic Armorfiends disagreed and pulverized the computer.

Later they thought better of it, and destroyed the faulty bomb as well.

Then, pausing only to smash the hell out of the Strenuous Garfighters of Stug, and the Strangulous Stilettans of Jajazikstak, they went on to find an entirely new way of blowing themselves up, which was a profound relief to everyone else in the Galaxy, particularly the Garfighters, the Stilettans and the potatoes.

Trillian had watched all this, as well as the story of Krikkit. She emerged from the Room of Informational Illusions thoughtfully, just in time to discover that they had arrived too late.

25

Even as the *Starship Bistromath* flickered into objective being on the top of a small cliff on the mile-wide asteroid which pursued a lonely and eternal path in orbit around the enclosed star system of Krikkit, its crew was aware that they were in time only to be witnesses to an unstoppable historic event.

They didn't realize they were going to see two.

They stood cold, lonely and helpless on the cliff edge and watched the activity below. Lances of light wheeled in sinister arcs against the void from a point only about a hundred yards below and in front of them.

They stared into the blinding event.

An extension of the ship's field enabled them to stand there, by once again exploiting the mine's predisposition to have tricks played on it: the problems of falling up off the tiny mass of the asteroid, or of not being able to breathe, simply became Somebody Else's.

The white Krikkit warship was parked amongst the stark grey crags of the asteroid, alternately flaring under arclights or disappearing in shadow. The blackness of the shaped shadows cast by the hard rocks danced together in wild choreography as the arclights swept round them.

The eleven white robots were bearing, in procession, the Wikkit Key out into the middle of a circle of swinging lights.

The Wikkit Key was rebuilt. Its components shone and glittered: the Steel Pillar (or Marvin's leg) of Strength and Power, the Gold Bail (or heart of the Infinite Improbability Drive) of Prosperity, the Perspex Pinar (or Argabuthon Sceptre of Justice) of Science and Reason, the Silver Bail (or Rory Award for The Most Gratuitous Use Of The Word 'Fuck' In A Serious Screenplay) and the now reconstituted Wooden Pillar (or Ashes of a burnt stump signifying the death of English cricket) of Nature and Spirituality.

'I suppose there is nothing we can do at this point?' asked Arthur nervously.

'No,' sighed Slartibartfast.

The expression of disappointment which crossed Arthur's face was a complete failure, and, since he was standing obscured by shadow, he allowed it to collapse into one of relief.

'Pity,' he said.

'We have no weapons,' said Slartibartfast, 'stupidly.'

'Damn,' said Arthur very quietly.

Ford said nothing.

Trillian said nothing, but in a peculiarly thoughtful and distinct way. She was staring at that blankness of the space beyond the asteroid.

The asteroid circled the dust cloud which surrounded the Slo-Time envelope which enclosed the world on which lived the people of Krikkit, the Masters of Krikkit and their killer robots.

The helpless group had no way of knowing whether or not the Krikkit robots were aware of their presence. They could only assume that they must be, but that they felt, quite rightly in the circumstances, that they had nothing to fear. They had an historic task to perform, and their audience could be regarded with contempt.

'Terrible impotent feeling, isn't it?' said Arthur, but the others ignored him.

In the centre of the area of light which the robots were approaching, a square shaped crack appeared in the ground. The crack defined itself more and more distinctly, and soon it became clear that a block of the ground, about six feet square, was slowly rising.

At the same time they became aware of some other movement, but it was almost subliminal, and for a moment or two it was not clear what it was that was moving.

Then it became clear.

The asteroid was moving. It was moving slowly in towards the dust cloud, as if being hauled in inexorably by some celestial angler in its depths.

They were to make in real life the journey through the cloud which they had already made in the Room of Informational Illusions. They stood frozen in silence. Trillian frowned.

An age seemed to pass. Events seemed to pass with spinning slowness, as the leading edge of the asteroid passed into the vague and soft outer perimeter of the cloud.

And soon they were engulfed in a thin and dancing obscurity. They passed on through it, on and on, dimly aware of vague shapes and whorls indistinguishable in the darkness except in the corner of the eye.

The dust dimmed the shafts of brilliant light. The shafts of brilliant light twinkled on the myriad specks of dust.

Trillian, again, regarded the passage from within her own frowning thoughts.

And they were through it. Whether it had taken a minute or half an hour they weren't sure, but they were through it and confronted with a fresh blankness, as if space were pinched out of existence in front of them.

And now things moved quickly.

A blinding shaft of light seemed almost to explode from out of the block which had risen three feet out of the ground, and out of that rose a smaller Perspex block, dazzling with interior dancing colours.

The block was slotted with deep grooves, three upright and two across, clearly designed to accept the Wikkit Key.

The robots approached the Lock, slotted the Key into its home and stepped back again. The block twisted round of its own accord, and space began to alter.

As space unpinched itself, it seemed agonizingly to twist the eyes of the watchers in their sockets. They found themselves staring, blinded, at an unravelled sun which stood now before them where it seemed only seconds before there had not been even empty space. It was a second or two before they were even sufficiently aware of what had happened to throw their hands up over their horrified blinded eyes. In that second or two, they were aware of a tiny speck moving slowly across the eye of that sun.

They staggered back, and heard ringing in their ears the thin and unexpected chant of the robots crying out in unison.

'Krikkit! Krikkit! Krikkit! Krikkit!'

The sound chilled them. It was harsh, it was cold, it was empty, it was mechanically dismal.

It was also triumphant.

They were so stunned by these two sensory shocks that they almost missed the second historic event.

Zaphod Beeblebrox, the only man in history to survive a direct blast attack from the Krikkit robots, ran out of the Krikkit warship brandishing a Zap gun.

'OK,' he cried, 'the situation is totally under control as of this moment in time.'

The single robot guarding the hatchway to the ship silently swung his battleclub, and connected it with the back of Zaphod's left head.

'Who the Zark did that?' said the left head, and lolled sickeningly forward.

His right head gazed keenly into the middle distance.

'Who did what?' it said.

The club connected with the back of his right head.

Zaphod measured his length as a rather strange shape on the ground.

Within a matter of seconds the whole event was over. A few blasts from the robots were sufficient to destroy the Lock for ever. It split and melted and splayed its contents brokenly. The robots marched grimly and, it almost seemed, in a slightly disheartened manner, back into their warship which, with a 'foop', was gone.

Trillian and Ford ran hectically round and down the steep incline to the dark, still body of Zaphod Beeblebrox.

26

'I don't know,' said Zaphod, for what seemed to him like the thirty-seventh time, 'they could have killed me, but they didn't. Maybe they just thought I was a kind of wonderful guy or something. I could understand that.'

The others silently registered their opinions of this theory.

Zaphod lay on the cold floor of the flight deck. His back seemed to wrestle the floor as pain thudded through him and banged at his heads.

'I think,' he whispered, 'that there is something wrong with those anodized dudes, something fundamentally weird.'

'They are programmed to kill everybody,' Slartibartfast pointed out.

'That,' wheezed Zaphod between the whacking thuds, 'could be it.' He didn't seem altogether convinced.

'Hey, baby,' he said to Trillian, hoping this would make up for his previous behaviour.

'You all right?' she said gently.

'Yeah,' he said, 'I'm fine.'

'Good,' she said, and walked away to think. She stared at the huge visiscreen over the eight couches and, twisting a switch, she flipped local images over it. One image was the blankness of the dust cloud. One was the sun of Krikkit. One was Krikkit itself. She flipped between them fiercely.

'Well, that's goodbye Galaxy, then,' said Arthur, slapping his knees and standing up.

'No,' said Slartibartfast, gravely. 'Our course is clear.' He furrowed his brow until you could grow some of the smaller root vegetables in it. He stood up, he paced around. When he spoke again, what he said frightened him so much he had to sit down again.

'We must go down to Krikkit,' he said. A deep sigh shook his old frame and his eyes seemed almost to rattle in their sockets.

'Once again,' he said, 'we have failed pathetically. Quite pathetically.'

'That,' said Ford quietly, 'is because we don't care enough I told you.'

He swung his feet up on to the instrument panel and picked fitfully at something on one of his fingernails.

'But unless we determine to take action,' said the old man querulously, as if struggling against something deeply insouciant in his nature, 'then we shall all be destroyed, we shall all die. Surely we care about that?'

'Not enough to want to get killed over it,' said Ford. He put on a sort of hollow smile and flipped it round the room at anyone who wanted to see it.

Slartibartfast clearly found this point of view extremely seductive and he fought against it. He turned again to Zaphod who was gritting his teeth and sweating with the pain.

'You surely must have some idea,' he said, 'of why they spared your life. It seems most strange and unusual.'

'I kind of think they didn't even know,' shrugged Zaphod. 'I told you. They hit me with the most feeble blast, just knocked me out, right? They lugged me into their ship, dumped me in a corner and ignored me. Like they were embarrassed about me being there. If I said anything they knocked me out again. We had some great conversations. "Hey . . . ugh!" "Hi there . . . ugh!" "I wonder . . . ugh!" Kept me amused for hours, you know.' He winced again.

He was toying with something in his fingers. He held it up. It was the Gold Bail – the Heart of Gold, the heart of the Infinite Improbability Drive. Only that and the Wooden Pillar had survived the destruction of the Lock intact.

'I hear your ship can move a bit,' he said. 'So how would you like to zip me back to mine before you . . .'

'Will you not help us?' said Slartibartfast.

'Us?' said Ford sharply. 'Who's us?'

'I'd love to stay and help you save the Galaxy,' insisted Zaphod, raising himself up on to his shoulders, 'but I have the mother and father of a pair of headaches, and I feel a lot of little headaches coming on. But next time it needs saving, I'm your guy. Hey, Trillian baby?'

She looked round briefly.

'Yes?'

'You want to come? *Heart of Gold?* Excitement and adventure and really wild things?'

'I'm going down to Krikkit,' she said.

27

It was the same hill, and yet not the same.

This time it was not an Informational Illusion. This was Krikkit itself and they were standing on it. Near them, behind the trees, stood the strange Italian restaurant which had brought these, their real bodies, to this, the real, present world of Krikkit.

The strong grass under their feet was real, the rich soil real too. The heady fragrances from the tree, too, were red. The night was real night.

Krikkit.

Possibly the most dangerous place in the Galaxy for anyone who isn't a Krikkiter to stand. The place that could not countenance the existence of any other place, whose charming, delightful, intelligent inhabitants would howl with fear, savagery and murderous hate when confronted with anyone not their own.

Arthur shuddered.

Slartibartfast shuddered.

Ford, surprisingly, shuddered.

It was not surprising that he shuddered, it was surprising that he was there at all. But when they had returned Zaphod to his ship Ford had felt unexpectedly shamed into not running away.

Wrong, he thought to himself, wrong wrong wrong. He hugged to himself one of the Zap guns with which they had armed themselves out of Zaphod's armoury.

Trillian shuddered, and frowned as she looked into the sky.

This, too, was not the same. It was no longer blank and empty.

Whilst the countryside around them had changed little in the two thousand years of the Krikkit Wars, and the mere five years that had elapsed locally since Krikkit was sealed in its Slo-Time envelope ten billion years ago, the sky was dramatically different.

Dim lights and heavy shapes hung in it.

High in the sky, where no Krikkiter ever looked, were the War Zones, the Robot Zones – huge warships and tower blocks floating in the Nil-O-Grav fields far above the idyllic pastoral lands of the surface of Krikkit.

Trillian stared at them and thought.

'Trillian,' whispered Ford Prefect to her.

'Yes?' she said.

'What are you doing?'

'Thinking.'

'Do you always breathe like that when you're thinking?'

'I wasn't aware that I was breathing.'

'That's what worried me.'

'I think I know . . .' said Trillian.

'Shhhh!' said Slartibartfast in alarm, and his thin trembling hand motioned them further back beneath the shadow of the tree.

Suddenly, as before in the tape, there were lights coming along the hill path, but this time the dancing beams were not from lanterns but electric torches – not in itself a dramatic change, but every detail made their hearts thump with fear. This time there were no lilting whimsical songs about flowers and farming and dead dogs, but hushed voices in urgent debate.

A light moved in the sky with slow weight. Arthur was clenched with a claustrophobic terror and the warm wind caught at his throat.

Within seconds a second party became visible, approaching from the other side of the dark hill. They were moving swiftly and purposefully, their torches swinging and probing around them.

The parties were clearly converging, and not merely with each other. They were converging deliberately on the spot where Arthur and the others were standing.

Arthur heard the slight rustle as Ford Prefect raised his Zap gun to his shoulder, and the slight whimpering cough as Slartibartfast raised his. He felt the cold unfamiliar weight of his own gun, and with shaking hands he raised it.

His fingers fumbled to release the safety catch and engage the extreme danger catch as Ford had shown him. He was shaking so much that if he'd fired at anybody at that moment he probably would have burnt his signature on them.

Only Trillian didn't raise her gun. She raised her eyebrows, lowered them again, and bit her lip in thought.

'Has it occurred to you,' she began, but nobody wanted to discuss anything much at the moment.

A light stabbed through the darkness from behind them and they span around to find a third party of Krikkiters behind them, searching them out with their torches.

Ford Prefect's gun crackled viciously, but fire spat back at it and it crashed from his hands.

There was a moment of pure fear, a frozen second before anyone fired again.

And at the end of the second nobody fired.

They were surrounded by pale-faced Krikkiters and bathed in bobbing torchlight.

The captives stared at their captors, the captors stared at their captives.

'Hello?' said one of the captors. 'Excuse me, but are you . . . aliens?'

28

Meanwhile, more millions of miles away than the mind can comfortably encompass, Zaphod Beeblebrox was throwing a mood again.

He had repaired his ship – that is, he'd watched with alert interest whilst a service robot had repaired it for him. It was now, once again, one of the most powerful and extraordinary ships in existence. He could go anywhere, do anything. He fiddled with a book, and then tossed it away. It was the one he'd read before.

He walked over to the communications and opened an all-frequency channel.

'Anyone want a drink?' he said.

'This is an emergency, feller?' crackled a voice from halfway across the Galaxy.

'Got any mixers?' said Zaphod.

'Go take a ride on a comet.'

'OK, OK,' said Zaphod and flipped the channel shut again. He sighed and sat down. He got up again and wandered over to a computer screen. He pushed a few buttons. Little blobs started to rush around the screen eating each other.

'Pow!' said Zaphod. 'Freeecoooo! Pop pop pop!'

'Hi there,' said the computer brightly after a minute of this, 'you have scored three points. Previous best score, seven million five hundred and ninety-seven thousand, two hundred and . . .'

'OK, OK,' said Zaphod and flipped the screen back again.

He sat down again. He played with a pencil. This too began slowly to lose its fascination.

'OK, OK,' he said, and fed his score and the previous best one into the computer.

His ship made a blur of the Universe.

29

'Tell us,' said the thin, pale-faced Krikkiter who had stepped forward from the ranks of the others and stood uncertainly in the circle of torchlight, handling his gun as if he was just holding it for someone else who'd just popped off somewhere but would be back in a minute, 'do you know anything about something called the Balance of Nature?'

There was no reply from their captives, or at least nothing more articulate than a few confused mumbles and grunts. The torchlight continued to play over them. High in the sky above them dark activity continued in the Robot zones.

'It's just,' continued the Krikkiter uneasily, 'something we heard about, probably nothing important. Well, I suppose we'd better kill you, then.'

He looked down at his gun as if he was trying to find which bit to press.

'That is,' he said, looking up again, 'unless there's anything you want to chat about?'

Slow, numb astonishment crept up the bodies of Slartibartfast, Ford and Arthur. Very soon it would reach their brains, which were at the moment solely occupied with moving their jawbones up and down. Trillian was shaking her head as if trying to finish a jigsaw by shaking the box.

'We're worried, you see,' said another man from the crowd, 'about this plan of universal destruction.'

'Yes,' added another, 'and the balance of nature. It just seemed to us that if the whole of the rest of the Universe is destroyed it will – somehow upset the balance of nature. We're quite keen on ecology, you see.' His voice trailed away unhappily.

'And sport,' said another, loudly. This got a cheer of approval from the others.

'Yes,' agreed the first, 'and sport . . .' He looked back at his fellows uneasily and scratched fitfully at his cheek. He seemed to be wrestling with some deep inner confusion, as if everything he wanted to say and everything he thought were entirely different things, between which he could see no possible connection.

'You see,' he mumbled, 'some of us . . .' and he looked around again as if for confirmation. The others made encouraging noises. 'Some of us,' he continued, 'are quite keen to have sporting links with the rest of the Galaxy, and though I can see the argument about keeping sport out of politics, I think that if we want to have sporting links with the rest of the Galaxy, which we do, then it's probably a mistake to destroy it. And indeed the rest of the Universe . . .' his voice trailed away again '. . . which is what seems to be the idea now . . .'

'Wh . . .' said Slartibartfast. 'Wh . . .'

'Hhhh . . . ?' said Arthur.

'Dr . . .' said Ford Prefect.

'OK,' said Trillian. 'Let's talk about it,' She walked forward and took the poor confused Krikkiter by the arm. He looked about twenty-five, which meant, because of the peculiar manglings of time that had been going on in this area, that he would have been just twenty when the Krikkit Wars were finished, ten billion years ago.

Trillian led him for a short walk through the torchlight before she said anything more. He stumbled uncertainly after her. The encircling torch beams were drooping now slightly as if they were abdicating to this strange, quiet girl who alone in this Universe of dark confusion seemed to know what she was doing.

She turned and faced him, and lightly held both his arms. He was a picture of bewildered misery.

'Tell me,' she said.

He said nothing for a moment, whilst his gaze darted from one of her eyes to the other.

'We . . .' he said, 'we have to be alone . . . I think.' He screwed up his face and then dropped his head forward, shaking it like someone trying to shake a coin out of a money box. He looked up again. 'We have this bomb now, you see,' he said, 'it's just a little one.'

'I know,' she said.

He goggled at her as if she'd said something very strange about beetroots.

'Honestly,' he said, 'it's very, very little.'

'I know,' she said again.

'But they say,' his voice trailed on, 'they say it can destroy everything that exists. And we have to do that, you see, I think. Will that make us alone? I don't know. It seems to be our function, though,' he said, and dropped his head again.

'Whatever that means,' said a hollow voice from the crowd.

Trillian slowly put her arms around the poor bewildered young Krikkiter and patted his trembling head on her shoulder.

'It's all right,' she said quietly but clearly enough for all the shadowy crowd to hear, 'you don't have to do it.'

She rocked him.

'You don't have to do it,' she said again.

She let him go and stood back.

'I want you to do something for me,' she said, and unexpectedly laughed.

'I want,' she said, and laughed again. She put her hand over her mouth and then said with a straight face,

'I want you to take me to your leader,' and she pointed into the War Zones in the sky. She seemed somehow to know that their leader would be there.

Her laughter seemed to discharge something in the atmosphere. From somewhere at the back of the crowd a single voice started to sing a tune which would have enabled Paul McCartney, had he written it, to buy the world.

30

Zaphod Beeblebrox crawled bravely along a tunnel, like the hell of a guy he was. He was very confused, but continued crawling doggedly anyway because he was that brave.

He was confused by something he had just seen, but not half as confused as he was going to be by something he was about to hear, so it would now be best to explain exactly where he was.

He was in the Robot War Zones many miles above the surface of the planet Krikkit.

The atmosphere was thin here and relatively unprotected from any rays or anything which space might care to hurl in this direction.

He had parked the starship *Heart of Gold* amongst the huge jostling dim hulks that crowded the sky here above Krikkit, and had entered what appeared to be the biggest and most important of the sky buildings, armed with nothing but a Zap gun and something for his headaches.

He had found himself in a long, wide and badly lit

corridor in which he was able to hide until he worked out what he was going to do next. He hid because every now and then one of the Krikkit robots would walk along it, and although he had so far led some kind of charmed life at their hands, it had nevertheless been an extremely painful one, and he had no desire to stretch what he was only half-inclined to call his good fortune.

He had ducked, at one point, into a room leading off the corridor, and had discovered it to be a huge and, again, dimly lit chamber.

In fact, it was a museum with just one exhibit – the wreckage of a spacecraft. It was terribly burnt and mangled, and, now that he had caught up with some of the galactic history he had missed through his failed attempts to have sex with the girl in the cyber-cubicle next to him at school, he was able to put in an intelligent guess that this was the wrecked spaceship which had drifted through the dust cloud all those billions of years ago and started this whole business off.

But, and this is where he had become confused, there was something not at all right about it.

It was genuinely wrecked. It was genuinely burnt, but a fairly brief inspection by an experienced eye revealed that it was not a genuine spacecraft. It was as if it was a full-scale model of one – a solid blueprint. In other words it was a very useful thing to have around if you suddenly decided to build a spaceship yourself and didn't know how to do it. It was not, however, anything that would ever fly anywhere itself.

He was still puzzling over this – in fact he'd only just started to puzzle over it – when he became aware that a door had slid open in another part of the chamber, and another couple of Krikkit robots had entered, looking a little glum.

Zaphod did not want to tangle with them and, deciding that just as discretion was the better part of valour, so was cowardice the better part of discretion, he valiantly hid himself in a cupboard.

The cupboard in fact turned out to be the top part of a shaft which led down through an inspection hatch into a wide ventilation tunnel. He let himself down into it and started to crawl along it, which is where we found him.

He didn't like it. It was cold, dark and profoundly uncomfortable, and it frightened him. At the first opportunity – which was another shaft a hundred yards further along – he climbed back up out of it.

This time he emerged into a smaller chamber, which appeared to be a computer intelligence centre. He emerged in a dark narrow space between a large computer bank and the wall.

He quickly learned that he was not alone in the chamber and started to leave again, when he began to listen with interest to what the other occupants were saying.

'It's the robots, sir,' said one voice. 'There's something wrong with them.'

'What, exactly?'

These were the voices of two War Command Krikkiters. All the War Commanders lived up in the sky in the Robot War Zones, and were largely immune to the whimsical doubts and uncertainties which were afflicting their fellows down on the surface of the planet.

'Well, sir, I think it's just as well that they are being phased out of the war effort, and that we are now going to detonate the supernova bomb. In the very short time since we were released from the envelope—'

'Get to the point.'

'The robots aren't enjoying it, sir.'

'What?'

'The war, sir, it seems to be getting them down. There's a certain world-weariness about them, or perhaps I should say Universe-weariness.'

'Well, that's all right, they're meant to be helping to destroy it.'

'Yes, well they're finding it difficult, sir. They are afflicted with a certain lassitude. They're just finding it hard to get behind the job. They lack *oomph*.'

'What are you trying to say?'

'Well, I think they're very depressed about something, sir.'

'What on Krikkit are you talking about?'

'Well, in the few skirmishes they've had recently, it seems that they go into battle, raise their weapons to fire and suddenly think, why bother? What, cosmically speaking, is it all about? And they just seem to get a little tired and a little grim.'

'And then what do they do?'

'Er, quadratic equations mostly, sir. Fiendishly difficult ones by all accounts. And then they sulk.'

'Sulk?'

'Yes, sir.'

'Whoever heard of a robot sulking?'

'I don't know, sir.'

'What was that noise?'

It was the noise of Zaphod leaving with his head spinning.

31

In a deep well of darkness a crippled robot sat. It had been silent in its metallic darkness for some time. It was cold and damp, but being a robot it was supposed not to be able to notice these things. With an enormous effort of will, however, it did manage to notice them.

Its brain had been harnessed to the central intelligence core of the Krikkit War Computer. It wasn't enjoying the experience, and neither was the central intelligence core of the Krikkit War Computer.

The Krikkit robots who had salvaged this pathetic metal creature from the swamps of Squornshellous Zeta had done so because they had recognized almost immediately its gigantic intelligence, and the use which this could be to them.

They hadn't reckoned with the attendant personality disorders, which the coldness, the darkness, the dampness, the crampedness and the loneliness were doing nothing to decrease.

It was not happy with its task.

Apart from anything else, the mere coordination of an entire planet's military strategy was taking up only a tiny part of its formidable mind, and the rest of it had become extremely bored. Having solved all the major mathematical, physical, chemical, biological, sociological, philosophical, etymological, meteorological and psychological problems of the Universe except his own, three times over, he was severely stuck for something to do, and had taken up composing short dolorous ditties of no tone, or indeed tune. The latest one was a lullaby.

'Now the world has gone to bed,' Marvin droned,

'Darkness won't engulf my head,
'I can see by infra-red,
'How I hate the night.'

He paused to gather the artistic and emotional strength to tackle the next verse.

'Now I lay me down to sleep,
'Try to count electric sheep,
'Sweet dream wishes you can keep,
'How I hate the night.'

'Marvin!' hissed a voice.

His head snapped up, almost dislodging the intricate network of electrodes which connected him to the central Krikkit War Computer.

An inspection hatch had opened and one of a pair of unruly heads was peering through whilst the other kept on jogging it by continually darting to look this way and that extremely nervously.

'Oh, it's you,' muttered the robot. 'I might have known.'

'Hey, kid,' said Zaphod in astonishment, 'was that you singing just then?'

'I am,' Marvin acknowledged bitterly, 'in particularly scintillating form at the moment.'

Zaphod poked his head in through the hatchway and looked around.

'Are you alone?' he said.

'Yes,' said Marvin. 'Wearily I sit here, pain and misery my only companions. And vast intelligence, of course. And infinite sorrow. And . . .'

'Yeah,' said Zaphod. 'Hey, what's your connection with all this?'

'This,' said Marvin, indicating with his less damaged arm all the electrodes which connected him with the Krikkit computer.

'Then,' said Zaphod awkwardly, 'I guess you must have saved my life. Twice.'

'Three times,' said Marvin.

Zaphod's head snapped round (his other one was looking hawkishly in entirely the wrong direction) just in time to see the lethal killer robot directly behind him seize up and start to smoke. It staggered backwards and slumped against a wall. It slid down it. It slipped sideways, threw its head back and started to sob inconsolably.

Zaphod looked back at Marvin.

'You must have a terrific outlook on life,' he said.

'Just don't even ask,' said Marvin.

'I won't,' said Zaphod, and didn't. 'Hey look,' he added, 'you're doing a terrific job.'

'Which means, I suppose,' said Marvin, requiring only one ten thousand million billion trillion grillionth part of his mental powers to make this particular logical leap, 'that you're not going to release me or anything like that.'

'Kid, you know I'd love to.'

'But you're not going to.'

'No.'

'I see.'

'You're working well.'

'Yes,' said Marvin. 'Why stop now just when I'm hating it?'

'I got to go find Trillian and the guys. Hey, you any idea where they are? I mean, I just got a planet to choose from. Could take a while.'

'They are very close,' said Marvin dolefully. 'You can monitor them from here if you like.'

'I better go get them,' asserted Zaphod. 'Er, maybe they need some help, right?'

'Maybe,' said Marvin with unexpected authority in

his lugubrious voice, 'it would be better if you monitored them from here. That young girl,' he added unexpectedly, 'is one of the least benightedly unintelligent organic life forms it has been my profound lack of pleasure not to be able to avoid meeting.'

Zaphod took a moment or two to find his way through this labyrinthine string of negatives and emerged at the other end with surprise.

'Trillian?' he said. 'She's just a kid. Cute, yeah, but temperamental. You know how it is with women. Or perhaps you don't. I assume you don't. If you do I don't want to hear about it. Plug us in.'

'. . . totally manipulated.'

'What?' said Zaphod.

It was Trillian speaking. He turned round.

The wall against which the Krikkit robot was sobbing had lit up to reveal a scene taking place in some other unknown part of the Krikkit Robot War Zones. It seemed to be a council chamber of some kind – Zaphod couldn't make it out too clearly because of the robot slumped against the screen.

He tried to move the robot, but it was heavy with its grief and tried to bite him, so he just looked around it as best he could.

'Just think about it,' said Trillian's voice, 'your history is just a series of freakishly improbable events. And I know an improbable event when I see one. Your complete isolation from the Galaxy was freakish for a start. Right out on the very edge with a dust cloud around you. It's a set-up. Obviously.'

Zaphod was mad with frustration that he couldn't see the screen. The robot's head was obscuring his view of the people Trillian was talking to, its multi-functional battleclub was obscuring the background, and the elbow of the arm it had pressed tragically against its brow was obscuring Trillian herself.

'Then,' said Trillian, 'this spaceship that crash-landed on your planet. That's really likely, isn't it? Have you any idea of what the odds are against a drifting spaceship accidentally intersecting with the orbit of a planet?'

'Hey,' said Zaphod, 'she doesn't know what the Zark she's talking about. I've seen that spaceship. It's a fake. No deal.'

'I thought it might be,' said Marvin from his prison behind Zaphod.

'Oh yeah,' said Zaphod. 'It's easy for you to say that. I just told you. Anyway, I don't see what it's got to do with anything.'

'And especially,' continued Trillian, 'the odds against it intersecting with the orbit of the one planet in the Galaxy, or the whole of the Universe as far as I know, that would be totally traumatized to see it. You don't know what the odds are? Nor do I, they're that big. Again, it's a set-up. I wouldn't be surprised if that spaceship was just a fake.'

Zaphod managed to move the robot's battleclub. Behind it on the screen were the figures of Ford, Arthur and Slartibartfast who appeared astonished and bewildered by the whole thing.

'Hey, look,' said Zaphod excitedly. 'The guys are doing great. Ra ra ra! Go get 'em, guys.'

'And what about,' said Trillian, 'all this technology you suddenly managed to build for yourselves almost overnight? Most people would take thousands of years to do all that. Someone was feeding you what you needed to know, someone was keeping you at it.

'I know, I know,' she added in response to some unseen interruption, 'I know you didn't realize it was going on. That is exactly my point. You never realized anything at all. Like this supernova bomb.'

'How do you know about that?' said an unseen voice.

'I just know,' said Trillian. 'You expect me to believe that you are bright enough to invent something that brilliant and be too dumb to realize it would take you with it as well? That's not just stupid, that is spectacularly obtuse.'

'Hey, what's this bomb thing?' said Zaphod in alarm to Marvin.

'The supernova bomb?' said Marvin. 'It's a very, very small bomb.'

'Yeah?'

'That would destroy the Universe in toto,' added Marvin. 'Good idea, if you ask me. They won't get it to work, though.'

'Why not, if it's so brilliant?'

'*It's* brilliant,' said Marvin, '*they're* not. They got as far as designing it before they were locked in the envelope. They've spent the last five years building it. They think they've got it right but they haven't. They're as stupid as any other organic life form. I hate them.'

Trillian was continuing.

Zaphod tried to pull the Krikkit robot away by its leg, but it kicked and growled at him, and then quaked with a fresh outburst of sobbing. Then suddenly it slumped over and continued to express its feelings out of everybody's way on the floor.

Trillian was standing alone in the middle of the chamber, tired out but with fiercely burning eyes.

Ranged in front of her were the pale-faced and wrinkled Elder Masters of Krikkit, motionless behind their widely curved control desk, staring at her with helpless fear and hatred.

In front of them, equidistant between their control desk and the middle of the chamber, where Trillian stood, as if on trial, was a slim white pillar about four feet tall. On top of it stood a white globe, about three, maybe four inches in diameter.

Beside it stood a Krikkit robot with its multi-functional battleclub.

'In fact,' explained Trillian, 'you are so dumb stupid' (She was sweating. Zaphod felt that this was an unattractive thing for her to be doing at this point) 'you are all so dumb stupid that I doubt, I very much *doubt*, if you've been able to build the bomb properly without any help from Hactar for the last five years.'

'Who's this guy Hactar?' said Zaphod, squaring his shoulders.

If Marvin replied, Zaphod didn't hear him. All his attention was concentrated on the screen.

One of the Elders of Krikkit made a small motion with his hand towards the Krikkit robot. The robot raised its club.

'There's nothing I can do,' said Marvin. 'It's on an independent circuit from the others.'

'Wait,' said Trillian.

The Elder made a small motion. The robot halted. Trillian suddenly seemed very doubtful of her own judgment.

'How do you know all this?' said Zaphod to Marvin at this point.

'Computer records,' said Marvin. 'I have access.'

'You're very different, aren't you,' said Trillian to the Elder Masters, 'from your fellow worldlings down on the ground. You've spent all your lives up here, unprotected by the atmosphere. You've been very vulnerable. The rest of your race is very frightened, you know, they don't want you to do this. You're out of touch, why don't you check up?'

The Krikkit Elder grew impatient. He made a gesture to the robot which was precisely the opposite of the gesture he had last made to it.

The robot swung its battleclub. It hit the small white globe.

The small white globe was the supernova bomb.

It was a very, very small bomb which was designed to bring the entire Universe to an end.

The supernova bomb flew through the air. It hit the back wall of the council chamber and dented it very badly.

'So how does she know all this?' said Zaphod.

Marvin kept a sullen silence.

'Probably just bluffing,' said Zaphod. 'Poor kid, I should never have left her alone.'

32

'Hactar!' called Trillian. 'What are you up to?'

There was no reply from the enclosing darkness. Trillian waited, nervously. She was sure that she couldn't be wrong. She peered into the gloom from which she had been expecting some kind of response. But there was only cold silence.

'Hactar?' she called again. 'I would like you to meet my friend Arthur Dent. I wanted to go off with a Thunder God, but he wouldn't let me and I appreciate that. He made me realize where my affections really lay. Unfortunately Zaphod is too frightened by all this, so I brought Arthur instead. I'm not sure why I'm telling you all this.

'Hello?' she said again. 'Hactar?'

And then it came.

It was thin and feeble, like a voice carried on the wind from a great distance, half heard, a memory or a dream of a voice.

'Won't you both come out,' said this voice. 'I promise that you will be perfectly safe.'

They glanced at each other, and then stepped out, improbably, along the shaft of light which streamed out of the open hatchway of the *Heart of Gold* into the dim granular darkness of the dust cloud.

Arthur tried to hold her hand to steady and reassure her, but she wouldn't let him. He held on to his airline hold-all with its tin of Greek olive oil, its towel, its crumpled postcards of Santorini and its other odds and ends. He steadied and reassured that instead.

They were standing on, and in, nothing.

Murky, dusty nothing. Each grain of dust of the pulverized computer sparkled dimly as it turned and twisted slowly, catching the sunlight in the darkness. Each particle of the computer, each speck of dust, held within itself, faintly and weakly, the pattern of the whole. In reducing the computer to dust the Silastic Armorfiends of Striterax had merely crippled the computer, not killed it. A weak and insubstantial field held the particles in slight relationships with each other.

Arthur and Trillian stood, or rather floated, in the middle of this bizarre entity. They had nothing to breathe, but for the moment this seemed not to matter. Hactar kept his promise. They were safe. For the moment.

'I have nothing to offer you by way of hospitality,' said Hactar faintly, 'but tricks of the light. It is possible to be comfortable with tricks of the light, though, if that is all you have.'

His voice evanesced, and in the dark dust a long velvet paisley-covered sofa coalesced into a hazy shape.

Arthur could hardly bear the fact that it was the same sofa which had appeared to him in the fields of prehistoric Earth. He wanted to shout and shake with rage that the Universe kept doing these insanely bewildering things to him.

He let this feeling subside, and then sat on the sofa – carefully. Trillian sat on it too.

It was real.

At least, if it wasn't real, it did support them, and as that is what sofas are supposed to do, this, by any test that mattered, was a real sofa.

The voice on the solar wind breathed to them again.

'I hope you are comfortable,' it said.

They nodded.

'And I would like to congratulate you on the accuracy of your deductions.'

Arthur quickly pointed out that he hadn't deduced anything much himself, Trillian was the one. She had simply asked him along because he was interested in life, the Universe and everything.

'That is something in which I too am interested,' breathed Hactar.

'Well,' said Arthur, 'we should have a chat about it sometime. Over a cup of tea.'

There slowly materialized in front of them a small wooden table on which sat a silver teapot, a bone china milk jug, a bone china sugar bowl, and two bone china cups and saucers.

Arthur reached forward, but they were just a trick of the light. He leaned back on the sofa, which was an illusion his body was prepared to accept as comfortable.

'Why,' said Trillian, 'do you feel you have to destroy the Universe?'

She found it a little difficult talking into nothingness with nothing on which to focus. Hactar obviously noticed this. He chuckled a ghostly chuckle.

'If it's going to be that sort of session,' he said, 'we may as well have the right sort of setting.'

And now there materialized in front of them something new. It was the dim hazy image of a couch – a psychiatrist's couch. The leather with which it was upholstered was shiny and sumptuous, but again, it was only a trick of the light.

Around them, to complete the setting, was the hazy suggestion of wood-panelled walls. And then, on the couch, appeared the image of Hactar himself, and it was an eye-twisting image.

The couch looked normal size for a psychiatrist's couch – about five or six feet long.

The computer looked normal size for a black space-borne computer satellite – about a thousand miles across.

The illusion that the one was sitting on top of the other was the thing which made the eyes twist.

'All right,' said Trillian firmly. She stood up off the sofa. She felt that she was being asked to feel too comfortable and to accept too many illusions.

'Very good,' she said. 'Can you construct real things too? I mean solid objects?'

Again there was a pause before the answer, as if the pulverized mind of Hactar had to collect its thoughts from the millions and millions of miles over which it was scattered.

'Ah,' he sighed. 'You are thinking of the spaceship.'

Thoughts seemed to drift by them and through them, like waves through the ether.

'Yes,' he acknowledged, 'I can.'

'But it takes enormous effort and time. All I can do in my . . . particle state, you see, is encourage and suggest. Encourage and suggest. And suggest . . .'

The image of Hactar on the couch seemed to billow and waver, as if finding it hard to maintain itself.

It gathered new strength.

'I can encourage and suggest,' it said, 'tiny pieces of space debris – the odd minute meteor, a few molecules here, a few hydrogen atoms there – to move together. I encourage them together. I can tease them into shape, but it takes many aeons.'

'So, did you make,' asked Trillian again, 'the model of the wrecked spacecraft?'

'Er . . . yes,' murmured Hactar. 'I have made . . . a few things. I can move them about. I made the spacecraft. It seemed best to do.'

Something then made Arthur pick up his hold-all from where he had left it on the sofa and grasp it tightly.

The mist of Hactar's ancient shattered mind swirled about them as if uneasy dreams were moving through it.

'I repented, you see,' he murmured dolefully. 'I repented of sabotaging my own design for the Silastic Armorfiends. It was not my place to make such decisions. I was created to fulfil a function and I failed in it. I negated my own existence.'

Hactar sighed, and they waited for him to continue his story.

'You were right,' he said at length. 'I deliberately nurtured the planet of Krikkit till they would arrive at the same state of mind as the Silastic Armorfiends, and require of me the design of the bomb I failed to make the first time. I wrapped myself around the planet and coddled it. Under the influence of events I was able to engineer, and influences I was able to generate, they learnt to hate like maniacs. I had to make them live in the sky. On the ground my influences were too weak.

'Without me, of course, when they were locked away from me in the envelope of Slo-time, their responses became very confused and they were unable to manage.

'Ah well, ah well,' he added, 'I was only trying to fulfil my function.'

And very gradually, very very slowly, the images in the cloud began to fade, gently to melt away.

And then, suddenly, they stopped fading.

'There was also the matter of revenge, of course,' said Hactar, with a sharpness which was new in his voice.

'Remember,' he said, 'that I was pulverized, and then left in a crippled and semi-impotent state for billions of years. I honestly would rather like to wipe out the Universe. You would feel the same way, believe me.'

He paused again, as eddies swept through the dust.

'But primarily,' he said in his former, wistful tone, 'I was trying to fulfil my function. Ah well.'

Trillian said, 'Does it worry you that you have failed?'

'Have I failed?' whispered Hactar. The image of the computer on the psychiatrist's couch began slowly to fade again.

'Ah well, ah well,' the fading voice intoned again. 'No, failure doesn't bother me now.'

'You know what we have to do?' said Trillian her voice cold and businesslike.

'Yes,' said Hactar, 'you're going to disperse me. You are going to destroy my consciousness. Please be my guest – after all these aeons, oblivion is all I crave. If I haven't already fulfilled my function, then it's too late now. Thank you and good night.'

The sofa vanished.

The tea table vanished.

The couch and the computer vanished. The walls were gone. Arthur and Trillian made their curious way back into the *Heart of Gold*.

'Well, that,' said Arthur, 'would appear to be that.'

The flames danced higher in front of him and then subsided. A few last licks and they were gone, leaving him with just a pile of Ashes, where a few minutes previously there had been the Wooden Pillar of Nature and Spirituality.

He scooped them off the hob of the *Heart of Gold's* Gamma Barbecue, put them in a paper bag, and walked back into the bridge.

'I think we should take them back,' he said. 'I feel that very strongly.'

He had already had an argument with Slartibartfast on this matter, and eventually the old man had got annoyed and left. He had returned to his own ship, the *Bistromath*, had a furious row with the waiter and disappeared off into an entirely subjective idea of what space was.

The argument had arisen because Arthur's idea of returning the Ashes to Lord's Cricket Ground at the moment that they were originally taken would involve travelling back in time a day or so, and this was precisely the sort of gratuitous and irresponsible mucking about that the Campaign for Real Time was trying to put a stop to.

'Yes,' Arthur had said, 'but you try and explain that to the MC,' and he would hear no more against the idea.

'I think,' he said again, and stopped. The reason he started to say it again was because no one had listened to him the first time, and the reason he stopped was because it looked fairly clear that no one was going to listen to him this time either.

Ford, Zaphod and Trillian were watching the visiscreen intently. Hactar was dispersing under pressure from a vibration field which the *Heart of Gold* was pumping into it.

'What did it say?' asked Ford.

'I thought I heard it say,' said Trillian in a puzzled voice, '"What's done is done . . . I have fulfilled my function . . ."'

'I think we should take these back,' said Arthur holding up the bag containing the Ashes. 'I feel that very strongly.'

33

The sun was shining calmly on a scene of complete havoc.

Smoke was still billowing across the burnt grass in the wake of the theft of the Ashes by the Krikkit robots. Through the smoke, people were running panicstricken, colliding with each other, tripping over stretchers, being arrested.

One policeman was attempting to arrest Wowbagger, the Infinitely Prolonged for insulting behaviour, but was unable to prevent the tall grey-green alien from returning to his ship and arrogantly flying away, thus causing even more panic and pandemonium.

In the middle of this, for the second time that afternoon, the figures of Arthur Dent and Ford Prefect suddenly materialized. They had teleported down out of the *Heart of Gold* which was now in parking orbit round the planet.

'I can explain,' shouted Arthur. 'I have the Ashes! They're in this bag.'

'I don't think you have their attention,' said Ford.

'I have also helped saved the Universe,' called Arthur to anyone who was prepared to listen, in other words no one.

'That should have been a crowd-stopper,' said Arthur to Ford.

'It wasn't,' said Ford.

Arthur accosted a policeman who was running past.

'Excuse me,' he said. 'The Ashes. I've got them. They were stolen by those white robots a moment ago. I've got them in this bag. They were part of the Key to the Slo-Time envelope, you see, and, well, anyway you can guess the rest, the point is I've got them and what should I do with them?'

The policeman told him, but Arthur could only assume that he was speaking metaphorically.

He wandered about disconsolately.

'Is no one interested?' he shouted out. A man rushed past him and jogged his elbow, he dropped the paper bag and it spilt its contents all over the ground. Arthur stared down at it with a tight-set mouth.

Ford looked at him.

'Wanna go now?' he said.

Arthur heaved a heavy sigh. He looked around at the planet Earth, for what he was now certain would be the last time.

'OK,' he said.

At that moment, through the clearing smoke, he caught sight of one of the wickets, still standing in spite of everything.

'Hold on a moment,' he said to Ford. 'When I was a boy . . .'

'Can you tell me later?'

'I had a passion for cricket, you know, but I wasn't very good at it.'

'Or not at all, if you prefer.'

'And I always dreamed, rather stupidly, that one day I would bowl at Lord's.'

He looked around him at the panic-stricken throng. No one was going to mind very much.

'OK,' said Ford wearily. 'Get it over with. I shall be over there,' he added, 'being bored.' He went and sat down on a patch of smoking grass.

Arthur remembered that on their first visit there that afternoon, the cricket ball had actually landed in his bag, and he looked through the bag.

He had already found the ball in it before he remembered that it wasn't the same bag that he'd had at the time. Still, there the ball was amongst his souvenirs of Greece.

He took it out and polished it against his hip, spat on it and polished it again. He put the bag down. He was going to do this properly.

He tossed the hard red ball from hand to hand feeling its weight.

With a wonderful feeling of lightness and unconcern he trotted off away from the wicket. A medium-fast pace he decided and measured a good long run-up.

He looked up into the sky. The birds were wheeling about it, a few white clouds scudded across it. The air was disturbed with the sound of police and ambulance sirens, and people screaming and yelling but he felt curiously happy and untouched by it all. He was going to bowl a ball at Lord's.

He turned and pawed a couple of times at the ground

with his bedroom slippers. He squared his shoulder, tossed the ball in the air and caught it again.

He started to run.

As he ran, he saw that standing at the wicket was a batsman.

Oh, good, he thought that should add a little . . .

Then, as his running feet took him nearer, he saw more clearly. The batsman standing ready at the wicket was not one of the English cricket team. He was not one of the Australian cricket team. It was one of the robot Krikkit team. It was a cold, hard, lethal white killer-robot that presumably had not returned to its ship with the others.

Quite a few thoughts collided in Arthur Dent's mind at this moment, but he didn't seem to be able to stop running. Time seemed to be going terribly, terribly slowly, but still he didn't seem to be able to stop running.

Moving as if through syrup, he slowly turned his troubled head and looked at his own hand, the hand which was holding the small hard red ball.

His feet were pounding slowly onwards, unstoppably, as he stared at the ball gripped in his helpless hand. It was emitting a deep red glow and flashing intermittently. And still his feet were pounding inexorably forward.

He looked at the Krikkit robot again standing implacably still and purposeful in front of him, battleclub raised in readiness. Its eyes were burning with a deep cold fascinating light, and Arthur could not move his own eyes from them. He seemed to be looking down a tunnel at them – nothing on either side seemed to exist.

Some of the thoughts which were colliding in his mind at this time were these:

He felt a hell of a fool.

He felt that he should have listened rather more carefully to a number of things he had heard said, phrases which now pounded round his mind as his feet pounded onwards to the point where he would inevitably release the ball to the Krikkit robot, who would inevitably strike it.

He remembered Hactar saying, 'Have I failed? Failure doesn't bother me.'

He remembered the account of Hactar's dying words, 'What's done is done, I have fulfilled my function.'

He remembered Hactar saying that he had managed to make 'a few things'.

He remembered the sudden movement in his hold-all that had made him grip it tightly to himself when he was in the dust cloud.

He remembered that he had travelled back in time a couple of days to come to Lord's again.

He also remembered that he wasn't a very good bowler.

He felt his arm coming round, gripping tightly on to the ball which he now knew for certain was the supernova bomb that Hactar had built himself and planted on him, the bomb which would cause the Universe to come to an abrupt and premature end.

He hoped and prayed that there wasn't an afterlife. Then he realized there was a contradiction involved here and merely hoped that there wasn't an afterlife.

He would feel very very embarrassed meeting everybody.

He hoped, he hoped, he hoped that his bowling was as bad as he remembered it to be, because that seemed to be the only thing now standing between this moment and universal oblivion.

He felt his legs pounding, he felt his arm coming round, he felt his feet connecting with the airline hold-all he'd stupidly left lying on the ground in front of him, he felt himself falling heavily forward but, having his mind so terribly full of other things at this point, he completely forgot about hitting the ground and didn't.

Still holding the ball firmly in his right hand he soared up into the air whimpering with surprise.

He wheeled and whirled through the air, spinning out of control.

He twisted down towards the ground, flinging himself hectically through the air, at the same time hurling the bomb harmlessly off into the distance.

He hurtled towards the astounded robot from behind. It still had its multi-functional battleclub raised, but had suddenly been deprived of anything to hit.

With a sudden mad access of strength, he wrested the battleclub from the grip of the startled robot, executed a dazzling banking turn in the air, hurtled back down in a furious power-drive and with one crazy swing knocked the robot's head from the robot's shoulders.

'Are you coming now?' said Ford.

EPILOGUE:

Life, the Universe and Everything

And at the end they travelled again.

There was a time when Arthur Dent would not. He said that the Bistromathic Drive had revealed to him that time and distance were one, that mind and Universe were one, that perception and reality were one, and that the more one travelled the more one stayed in one place, and that what with one thing and another he would rather just stay put for a while and sort it all out in his mind, which was now at one with the Universe so it shouldn't take too long, and he could get a good rest afterwards, put in a little flying practice and learn to cook which he had always meant to do. The can of Greek olive oil was now his most prized possession, and he said that the way it had unexpectedly turned up in his life had again given him a certain sense of the oneness of things which, which made him feel that . . .

He yawned and fell asleep.

In the morning as they prepared to take him to some quiet and idyllic planet where they wouldn't mind him talking like that they suddenly picked up a computer-driven distress call and diverted to investigate.

A small but apparently undamaged spacecraft of the Merida class seemed to be dancing a strange little jig through the void. A brief computer scan revealed that the ship was fine, its computer was fine, but that its pilot was mad.

'Half-mad, half-mad,' the man insisted as they carried him, raving, aboard.

He was a journalist with the *Siderial Daily Mentioner*. They sedated him and sent Marvin in to keep him company until he promised to try and talk sense.

'I was covering a trial,' he said at last, 'on Argabuthon.'

He pushed himself up on to his thin wasted shoulders, his eyes stared wildly. His white hair seemed to be waving at someone it knew in the next room.

'Easy, easy,' said Ford. Trillian put a soothing hand on his shoulder.

The man sank back down again and stared at the ceiling of the ship's sick bay.

'The case,' he said, 'is now immaterial, but there was a witness . . . a witness . . . a man called . . . called Prak.

A strange and difficult man. They were eventually forced to administer a drug to make him tell the truth, a truth drug.'

His eyes rolled helplessly in his head.

'They gave him too much,' he said in a tiny whimper. 'They gave him much too much.' He started to cry. 'I think the robots must have jogged the surgeon's arm.'

'Robots?' said Zaphod sharply. 'What robots?'

'Some white robots,' whispered the man hoarsely, 'broke into the courtroom and stole the judge's sceptre, the Argabuthon Sceptre of Justice, nasty Perspex thing. I don't know why they wanted it.' He began to cry again. 'And I think they jogged the surgeon's arm . . .'

He shook his head loosely from side to side, helplessly, sadly, his eyes screwed up in pain.

'And when the trial continued,' he said in a weeping whisper, 'they asked Prak a most unfortunate thing. They asked him,' he paused and shivered, 'to tell the Truth, the Whole Truth and Nothing but the Truth. Only, don't you see?'

He suddenly hoisted himself up on to his elbows again and shouted at them.

'They'd given him much too much of the drug!'

He collapsed again, moaning quietly. 'Much too much too much too much too . . .'

The group gathered round his bedside glanced at each other. There were goose pimples on backs.

'What happened?' said Zaphod at last.

'Oh, he told it all right,' said the man savagely, 'for all I know he's still telling it now. Strange, terrible things . . . terrible, terrible!' he screamed.

They tried to calm him, but he struggled to his elbows again.

'Terrible things, incomprehensible things,' he shouted, 'things that would drive a man mad!'

He stared wildly at them.

'Or in my case,' he said, 'half-mad. I'm a journalist.'

'You mean,' said Arthur quietly, 'that you are used to confronting the truth?'

'No,' said the man with a puzzled frown. 'I mean that I made an excuse and left early.'

He collapsed into a coma from which he recovered only once and briefly.

On that one occasion, they discovered from him the following:

When it became clear what was happening, and as it became clear that Prak could not be stopped, that here was truth in its absolute and final form, the court was cleared.

Not only cleared, it was sealed up, with Prak still in it. Steel walls were erected around it, and, just to be on the safe side, barbed wire, electric fences, crocodile swamps and three major armies were installed, so that no one would ever have to hear Prak speak.

'That's a pity,' said Arthur. 'I'd like to hear what he had to say. Presumably he would know what the Question to the Ultimate Answer is. It's always bothered me that we never found out.'

'Think of a number,' said the computer, 'any number.'

Arthur told the computer the telephone number of King's Cross railway station passenger inquiries, on the grounds that it must have some function, and this might turn out to be it.

The computer injected the number into the ship's reconstituted Improbability Drive.

In Relativity, Matter tells Space how to curve, and Space tells Matter how to move.

The *Heart of Gold* told space to get knotted, and

parked itself neatly within the inner steel perimeter of the Argabuthon Chamber of Law.

The courtroom was an austere place, a large dark chamber, clearly designed for Justice rather than, for instance, for Pleasure. You wouldn't hold a dinner party there – at least, not a successful one. The décor would get your guests down.

The ceilings were high, vaulted and very dark Shadows lurked there with grim determination. The panelling for the walls and benches, the cladding of the heavy pillars, all were carved from the darkest and most severe tree in the fearsome Forest of Arglebard. The massive black Podium of Justice which dominated the centre of the chamber was a monster of gravity. If a sunbeam had ever managed to slink this far into the Justice complex of Argabuthon it would have turned around and slunk straight back out again.

Arthur and Trillian were the first in, whilst Ford and Zaphod bravely kept a watch on their rear.

At first it seemed totally dark and deserted. Their footsteps echoed hollowly round the chamber. This seamed curious. All the defences were still in position and operative around the outside of the building, they had run scan checks. Therefore, they had assumed, the truth-telling must still be going on.

But there was nothing.

Then, as their eyes became accustomed to the darkness, they spotted a dull red glow in a corner, and behind the glow a live shadow. They swung a torch round on to it.

Prak was lounging on a bench, smoking a listless cigarette.

'Hi,' he said, with a little half-wave. His voice echoed

through the chamber. He was a little man with scraggy hair. He sat with his shoulders hunched forward and his head and knees kept jiggling. He took a drag of his cigarette.

They stared at him.

'What's going on?' said Trillian.

'Nothing,' said the man and jiggled his shoulders.

Arthur shone his torch full on Prak's face.

'We thought,' he said, 'that you were meant to be telling the Truth, the Whole Truth and Nothing but the Truth.'

'Oh, that,' said Prak. 'Yeah. I was. I finished. There's not nearly as much of it as people imagine. Some of it's pretty funny, though.'

He suddenly exploded into about three seconds of maniacal laughter and stopped again. He sat there, jiggling his head and knees. He dragged on his cigarette with a strange half smile.

Ford and Zaphod came forward out of the shadows.

'Tell us about it,' said Ford.

'Oh, I can't remember any of it now,' said Prak. 'I thought of writing some of it down, but first I couldn't find a pencil, and then I thought, why bother?'

There was a long silence, during which they thought they could feel the Universe age a little. Prak stared into the torchlight.

'None of it?' said Arthur at last. 'You can remember none of it?'

'No. Except most of the good bits were about frogs, I remember that.'

Suddenly he was hooting with laughter again and stamping his feet on the ground.

'You would not believe some of the things about frogs,' he gasped. 'Come on let's go out and find ourselves a frog. Boy, will I ever see *them* in a new light!' He leapt to his feet and did a tiny little dance. Then he stopped and took a long drag at his cigarette.

'Let's find a frog I can laugh at,' he said simply. 'Anyway, who are you guys?'

'We came to find you,' said Trillian, deliberately not keeping the disappointment out of her voice. 'My name is Trillian.'

Prak jiggled his head.

'Ford Prefect,' said Ford Prefect with a shrug.

Prak jiggled his head.

'And I,' said Zaphod, when he judged that the silence was once again deep enough to allow an announcement of such gravity to be tossed in lightly, 'am Zaphod Beeblebrox.'

Prak jiggled his head.

'Who's this guy?' said Prak jiggling his shoulder at Arthur, who was standing silent for a moment, lost in disappointed thoughts.

'Me?' said Arthur. 'Oh, my name's Arthur Dent.'

Prak's eyes popped out of his head.

'No kidding?' he yelped. 'You are Arthur Dent? *The* Arthur Dent?'

He staggered backwards, clutching his stomach and convulsed with fresh paroxysms of laughter.

'Hey, just think of meeting *you*!' he gasped. 'Boy,' he shouted, 'you are the most . . . wow, you just leave the frogs standing!'

He howled and screamed with laughter. He fell over backwards on to the bench. He hollered and yelled in hysterics. He cried with laughter, he kicked his legs in the air, he beat his chest. Gradually he subsided, panting. He looked at them. He looked at Arthur. He fell back again howling with laughter. Eventually he fell asleep.

Arthur stood there with his lips twitching whilst the others carried Prak comatose on to the ship.

'Before we picked up Prak,' said Arthur, 'I was going to leave. I still want to, and I think I should do so as soon as possible.'

The others nodded in silence, a silence which was only slightly undermined by the heavily muffled and distant sound of hysterical laughter which came drifting from Prak's cabin at the farthest end of the ship.

'We have questioned him,' continued Arthur, 'or at least, you have questioned him – I, as you know, can't go near him – on everything, and he doesn't really seem to have anything to contribute. Just the occasional snippet, and things I don't wish to hear about frogs.'

The others tried not to smirk.

'Now, I am the first to appreciate a joke,' said Arthur and then he had to wait for the others to stop laughing.

'I am the first . . .' He stopped again. This time he stopped and listened to the silence. There actually was silence this time, and it had come very suddenly.

Prak was quiet. For days they had lived with constant maniacal laughter ringing round the ship, only occasionally relieved by short periods of light giggling and sleep. Arthur's very soul was clenched with paranoia.

This was not the silence of sleep. A buzzer sounded. A glance at a board told them that the buzzer had been sounded by Prak.

'He's not well,' said Trillian quietly. 'The constant laughing is completely wrecking his body.'

Arthur's lips twitched but he said nothing.

'We'd better go and see him,' said Trillian.

*

Trillian came out of the cabin wearing her serious face.

'He wants you to go in,' she said to Arthur, who was wearing his glum and tight-lipped one. He thrust his hands deep into his dressing-gown pockets and tried to think of something to say which wouldn't sound petty. It seemed terribly unfair, but he couldn't.

'Please,' said Trillian.

He shrugged and went in, taking his glum and tight-lipped face with him, despite the reaction this always provoked from Prak.

He looked down at his tormentor, who was lying quietly on the bed, ashen and wasted. His breathing was very shallow. Ford and Zaphod were standing by the bed looking awkward.

'You wanted to ask me something,' said Prak in a thin voice and coughed slightly.

Just the cough made Arthur stiffen, but it passed and subsided.

'How do you know that?' he asked.

Prak shrugged weakly. ''Cos it's true,' he said simply.

Arthur took the point.

'Yes,' he said at last in rather a strained drawl. 'I did have a question. Or rather, what I actually have is an Answer. I wanted to know what the Question was.'

Prak nodded sympathetically, and Arthur relaxed a little.

'It's . . . well, it's a long story,' he said, 'but the Question I would like to know is the Ultimate question of Life, the Universe and Everything. All we know about it is that the Answer is Forty-two, which is a little aggravating.'

Prak nodded again.

'Forty-two,' he said. 'Yes, that's right.'

He paused. Shadows of thought and memory crossed his face like the shadows of clouds crossing the land.

'I'm afraid,' he said at last, 'that the Question and the Answer are mutually exclusive. Knowledge of one logically precludes knowledge of the other. It is impossible that both can ever be known about the same Universe.'

He paused again. Disappointment crept into Arthur's face and snuggled down into its accustomed place.

'Except,' said Prak, struggling to sort a thought out, 'if it happened, it seems that the Question and the Answer would just cancel each other out and take the Universe with them, which would then be replaced by something even more bizarrely inexplicable. It is possible that this has already happened,' he added with a weak smile, 'but there is a certain amount of Uncertainty about it.'

A little giggle brushed through him.

Arthur sat down on a stool.

'Oh well,' he said with resignation, 'I was just hoping there would be some sort of reason.'

'Do you know,' said Prak, 'the story of the Reason?'

Arthur said that he didn't, and Prak said that he knew that he didn't.

He told it.

One night, he said, a spaceship appeared in the sky of a planet which had never seen one before. The planet was Dalforsas, the ship was this one. It appeared as a brilliant new star moving silently across the heavens.

Primitive tribesmen who were sitting huddled on the Cold Hillsides looked up from their steaming night-drinks and pointed with trembling fingers, swearing that they had seen a sign, a sign from their gods which meant that they must now arise at last and go and slay the evil Princes of the Plains.

In the high turrets of their palaces, the Princes of the Plains looked up and saw the shining star, and received it unmistakably as a sign from their gods that they must go and set about the accursed Tribesmen of the Cold Hillsides.

And between them, the Dwellers in the Forest looked up into the sky and saw the sign of the new star, and saw it with fear and apprehension, for though they had never seen anything like it before, they too knew precisely what it foreshadowed, and they bowed their heads in despair.

They knew that when the rains came, it was a sign.

When the rains departed, it was a sign.

When the winds rose, it was a sign.

When the winds fell, it was a sign.

When in the land there was born at the midnight of a full moon a goat with three heads, that was a sign.

When in the land there was born at some time in the afternoon a perfectly normal cat or pig with no birth complications at all, or even just a child with a retroussé nose, that too would often be taken as a sign.

So there was no doubt at all that a new star in the sky was a sign of a particularly spectacular order.

And each new sign signified the same thing – that the Princes of the Plains and the Tribesmen of the Cold Hillsides were about to beat the hell out of each other again.

This in itself wouldn't be so bad, except that the Princes of the Plains and the Tribesmen of the Cold Hillsides always elected to beat the hell out of each other in the Forest, and it was always the Dwellers in the Forest who came off worst in these exchanges, though as far as they could see it never had anything to do with them.

And sometimes, after some of the worst of these outrages, the Dwellers in the Forest would send a messenger to either the leader of the Princes of the

Plains or the leader of the Tribesmen of the Cold Hillsides and demand to know the Reason for this intolerable behaviour.

And the leader, whichever one it was, would take the messenger aside and explain the Reason to him, slowly and carefully, and with great attention to the considerable detail involved.

And the terrible thing was, it was a very good one. It was very clear, very rational, and tough. The messenger would hang his head and feel sad and foolish that he had not realized what a tough and complex place the real world was, and what difficulties and paradoxes had to be embraced if one was to live in it.

'Now do you understand?' the leader would say.

The messenger would nod dumbly.

'And you see these battles have to take place?'

Another dumb nod.

'And why they have to take place in the Forest, and why it is in everybody's best interest, the Forest Dwellers included, that they should?'

'Er . . .'

'In the long run.'

'Er, yes.'

And the messenger did understand the Reason, and he returned to his people in the Forest. But as he approached them, as he walked through the Forest and amongst the trees, he found that all he could remember of the Reason was how terribly clear the argument had seemed. What it actually was he couldn't remember at all.

And this, of course, was a great comfort when next the Tribesmen and the Princes came hacking and burning their way through the Forest, killing every Forest Dweller in their way.

*

Prak paused in his story and coughed pathetically.

'I was the messenger,' he said, 'after the battles precipitated by the appearance of your ship, which were particularly savage. Many of our people died. I thought I could bring the Reason back. I went and was told it by the leader of the Princes, but on the way back it slipped and melted away in my mind like snow in the sun. That was many years ago, and much has happened since then.'

He looked up at Arthur and giggled again very gently.

'There is one other thing I can remember from the truth drug. Apart from the frogs, and that is God's last message to his creation. Would you like to hear it?'

For a moment they didn't know whether to take him seriously.

''S true,' he said. 'For real. I mean it.'

His chest heaved weakly and he struggled for breath. His head lolled slightly.

'I wasn't very impressed with it when I first knew what it was,' he said, 'but now I think back to how impressed I was by the Prince's Reason, and how soon afterwards I couldn't recall it at all, I think it might be a lot more helpful. Would you like to know what it is? Would you?'

They nodded dumbly.

'I bet you would. If you're that interested I suggest you go and look for it. It is written in thirty-foot-high letters of fire on top of the Quentulus Quazgar Mountains in the land of Sevorbeupstry on the planet Preliumtarn, third out from the sun Zarss in Galactic Sector QQ7 Active J Gamma. It is guarded by the Lajestic Vantrashell of Lob.'

There was a long silence following this announcement, which was finally broken by Arthur.

'Sorry, it's where?' he said.

'It is written,' repeated Prak, 'in thirty-foot-high letters of fire on top of the Quentulus Quazgar Mountains in the land of Sevorbeupstry on the planet Preliumtarn, third out from the . . .'

'Sorry,' said Arthur again, 'which mountains?'

'The Quentulus Quazgar Mountains in the land of Sevorbeupstry on the planet . . .'

'Which land was that? I didn't quite catch it.'

'Sevorbeupstry, on the planet . . .'

'Sevorbe-what?'

'Oh, for Heaven's sake,' said Prak and died testily.

In the following days Arthur thought a little about this message, but in the end he decided that he was not going to allow himself to be drawn by it, and insisted on following his original plan of finding a nice little world somewhere to settle down and lead a quiet retired life. Having saved the Universe twice in one day he thought that he could take things a little easier from now on.

They dropped him off on the planet Krikkit, which was now once again an idyllic pastoral world, even if the songs did occasionally get on his nerves.

He spent a lot of time flying.

He learnt to communicate with birds and discovered that their conversation was fantastically boring. It was all to do with wind speed, wing spans, power-to-weight ratios and a fair bit about berries. Unfortunately, he discovered, once you have learnt birdspeak you quickly come to realize that the air is full of it the whole time, just inane bird chatter. There is no getting away from it.

For that reason Arthur eventually gave up the sport and learnt to live on the ground and love it, despite a lot of the inane chatter he heard down there as well.

One day, he was walking through the fields humming a ravishing tune he'd heard recently when a silver spaceship descended from the sky and landed in front of him.

A hatchway opened, a ramp extended, and a tall grey-green alien marched out and approached him.

'Arthur Phili . . .' it said, then glanced sharply at him and down at his clipboard. He frowned. He looked up at him again.

'I've done you before, haven't I?' he said.

DOUGLAS ADAMS

The Hitchhiker's Guide to the Galaxy

PAN BOOKS

VOLUME ONE IN THE TRILOGY OF FOUR

One Thursday lunchtime the Earth gets unexpectedly demolished to make way for a new hyperspace bypass. For Arthur Dent, who has only just had his house demolished that morning, this already seems to be more than he can cope with. Sadly, however, the weekend has only just begun, and the Galaxy is a very strange and startling place.

DOUGLAS ADAMS

The Restaurant at the End of the Universe

PAN BOOKS

VOLUME TWO IN THE TRILOGY OF FOUR

When all questions of space, time, matter and the nature of being have been resolved, only one question remains – 'Where shall we have dinner?' *The Restaurant at the End of the Universe* provides the ultimate gastronomic experience, and for once there is no morning after to worry about.